The One and Only

MICHAEL JORDAN

He's the most electrifying player on the basketball court today as the superstar guard of the world champion Chicago Bulls, and the NBA's leading scorer since the 1986–87 season.

The statistics speak for themselves:

- He has scored more than 3,000 points in a single season (a distinction he shares with Wilt Chamberlain).

- He's the only NBA player to record 200 steals and 100 blocked shots in a season.

- He's a two-time Most Valuable Player and an All-Star since the day he came into the NBA in the 1984–85 season.

Follow this superstar on and off the court as this action-packed biography takes you from his boyhood to his heroics at the University of North Carolina and right through his amazing 1990–91 season!

Books by Bill Gutman

Sports Illustrated/BASEBALL'S RECORD BREAKERS
Sports Illustrated/GREAT MOMENTS IN BASEBALL
Sports Illustrated/GREAT MOMENTS IN PRO FOOTBALL
Sports Illustrated/PRO FOOTBALL'S RECORD BREAKERS
Sports Illustrated/STRANGE AND AMAZING BASEBALL
  STORIES
Sports Illustrated/STRANGE AND AMAZING FOOTBALL
  STORIES
BASEBALL SUPER TEAMS
BASEBALL'S HOT NEW STARS
BO JACKSON: A BIOGRAPHY
FOOTBALL SUPER TEAMS
GREAT SPORTS UPSETS
MICHAEL JORDAN: A BIOGRAPHY
PRO SPORTS CHAMPIONS
STRANGE AND AMAZING WRESTLING STORIES

Available from ARCHWAY Paperbacks

MICHAEL JORDAN
A BIOGRAPHY

BILL GUTMAN

AN ARCHWAY PAPERBACK
Published by POCKET BOOKS

New York London Toronto Sydney Tokyo Singapore

AN ARCHWAY PAPERBACK *Original*

An Archway Paperback published by
POCKET BOOKS, a division of Simon & Schuster Inc.
1230 Avenue of the Americas, New York, NY 10020

ISBN: 0-671-74932-3

First Archway Paperback printing December 1991

10 9 8 7 6 5 4

AN ARCHWAY PAPERBACK and colophon are registered trademarks of Simon & Schuster Inc.

Cover photos courtesy of *Sports Illustrated*

Printed in the U.S.A.

IL 5+

To a good friend and sports fan,
Dave Weiner

The author would like to thank both the Sports Information department at the University of North Carolina and the Public Relations department of the Chicago Bulls for furnishing background material useful in the preparation of this book.

Also, special thanks to Fred Lynch and Bill Guthridge for taking time to relate some personal reminiscences of their days with Michael Jordan.

Contents

CONTENTS

Part Three

Introduction

He is, without a doubt, the most electrifying basketball player of his time—and maybe any time. In fact, with each passing year more and more people are reaching this same conclusion. There is nothing that Michael Jordan cannot do on the basketball court. Whether it's one of his twisting, driving moves to the hoop, a gravity-defying slam-dunk, a sparkling pass, a long jump shot, or quick-handed steal, everything he does has a special kind of flair and verve that brings people to their feet, with smiles on their faces.

The overall brilliance of the Chicago Bulls' superstar can easily be reflected in the stats. Michael has been the league's scoring champion for five straight seasons through 1990–91. He has been voted the NBA's Most Valuable Player and Defensive Player of the Year for the same season. He's the only player, other than Wilt Chamberlain, to have scored more than 3,000 points in a single year, and he has reached the 10,000-point mark faster than any player in history except Chamberlain, who stood 7'1" and weighed about 275 pounds. He is also the only NBA player to record 200 steals and 100 blocked shots in the same season. He's been the league's slam-dunk champion and has been voted a starter on the All-Star team every year since his rookie season of 1984–85. His career scoring average of nearly 32.6 points a game is the highest in NBA history, as was his playoff average of 35.8 through the 1989–90 season.

Yet even a résumé like that doesn't really do justice to Michael Jordan. Numbers and awards are the substance. They don't necessarily talk about the style. Michael Jordan's greatness comes as much from his style as from his substance. For one thing, he is an absolute joy to watch on the basketball court. Not a game passes in which he doesn't do something that amazes everyone—fans, media, opponents, and teammates alike.

"Michael is just a great player, probably the greatest player who ever played," said Bulls' vice-president for basketball operations, Jerry Krause. "Because he is such a great competitor, even in practice, his teammates have a tendency to stand around and watch him during games. They sort of have that let-him-do-it attitude. It's hard not to be mesmerized by him."

There is simply an immense amount of talent packed into Michael's 6'6", 200-pound sinewy frame. He has a lightning-quick first step that enables him to blow past most defenders. Once he is airborne, his natural talent enables him to stay up for what seems like an inhuman length of time. Defensive players who leap with him are already on the way back to the floor while Michael Jordan continues to soar—faking, twisting, turning, and finally getting the shot away, sometimes from an almost impossible angle. More often than not, he drops it through the hoop.

But those gravity-defying drives aren't all he can do. Naturally, his great leaping ability makes it possible for him to slam-dunk. He can also pull up for the jumper and is even an accurate shooter from three-point range. In addition, Michael is a fine passer and has worked to make himself into a great defensive player. He has an uncanny instinct for the game and has the infinite ability to raise his level of play another notch at crunch time, when a game is on the line. Down the stretch, Michael Jordan can simply take over a ballgame.

That isn't all. It doesn't matter whether the Bulls are playing one of the best teams in the league or one of the worst, Michael Jordan plays the same way. He is "up" for every game and always projects the absolute joy of the sport to all those who see him. Unlike a lot of so-called superstars with huge, multiyear, multi-million-dollar contracts, Michael Jordan has never become complacent, has never coasted, and has never cheated himself, his fans, or teammates. He remains courteous and accessible, a highly visible commercial spokesman whose reputation as a "good guy" has never been tarnished. What you see is what you get: perhaps the greatest player to come down the hard-wood.

Yet with all his great individual skills, Michael Jordan has never stopped thinking *team*. His scoring average has slowly dropped as the players around him have become better. Even Michael himself has said:

This is what it's all about, the goal of every professional athlete. It took Michael Jordan and his Chicago Bulls teammates seven years to reach their goal of the NBA Championship. When it finally happened in June 1991, no one was prouder or happier than the sport's greatest player, Air Jordan. *(AP/Wide World Photo)*

"Individually, I don't think I have a thing left to prove to anyone. All I'm interested in is winning."

With Michael leading the way, the Bulls have slowly evolved into one of the NBA's elite teams, and in 1990–91, a championship team. The ballclub didn't become a winner until Michael's fourth season. By 1989–90, the team finished at 55-27, tied for the fifth-best record in the league, but only four games from the second-best. And in 1990–91, they not only won their division with a franchise-best 61-21 record, they also came within two games of having the best mark in all of professional basketball. Then in the playoffs, they swept past the defending-champion Detroit Pistons in the Eastern Conference finals, then whipped a veteran Los Angeles Laker team in five games to take their first-ever NBA crown.

In the eyes of many, the pro game continues to change and evolve. No longer does a team need a dominant center (à la Bill Russell, Wilt Chamberlain, Kareem Abdul-Jabbar) to be successful. Rather, they can build around players with all-around skills, such as Magic Johnson, Larry Bird, Clyde Drexler, Dominique Wilkins, or Charles Barkley. But the player who most epitomizes the modern-day superstar is Michael Jordan.

In fact, aside from the big men, it's always been the dynamic player with the all-around skills who mesmerizes the fans. First there was Bob Cousy, the legendary "Cooz" of the great Boston Celtics of the 1950s and 1960s. Next came Oscar Robertson, the "Big O," who at 6'5" had the skill to pass, shoot, play defense, and rebound. Then there was "Doctor J," Julius Erving, who electrified the fans with his seemingly impossible airborne tactics. After that came

Earvin "Magic" Johnson of the Lakers, a 6'9" point guard who combined the skills of the so-called little man with those of much bigger players.

And now there is Michael. Even Magic Johnson has conceded that the torch has been passed, that the man sometimes called "Air" Jordan has brought the game to another level.

"Everybody talks about how it's me and Larry [Bird]," Magic has said. "Really, there's Michael, and then there's everybody else."

PART

ONE

CHAPTER 1

Beginnings

It's hard to say how greatness evolves. No one can really predict which youngsters are going to be nuclear physicists, astronauts, brain surgeons, artists, or presidents. The same is true of athletes. Where does the greatness come from? Even the offspring of many great athletes have failed to approach the skill levels achieved by their fathers or mothers.

In Michael Jordan's case, basketball greatness did not come overnight. But once it began, it was like a crescendo that never stopped. When he started his high school career, Michael was considered a fine, all-around athlete and a good basketball player. By his junior year he began showing the star quality that ultimately resulted in his being recruited by the University of North Carolina.

Not only did he crack the starting lineup at Caroli-

3

na, but he also became the biggest hero in the state when his last-second jump shot gave the Tar Heels their first-ever national championship. Yet even with these heart-stopping heroics, he wasn't considered a superstar. That didn't come until the next year.

Michael achieved beyond expectations. He was voted College Player of the Year during his next two seasons, before deciding to forego his senior year for the professional ranks. Though he was the Bulls' first-round draft choice, no one expected Michael to make such a quick and complete transition to the pros. But once again he far exceeded everyone's expectations and began to become the dominant player of his time.

This was, however, not something that happened suddenly, and it certainly wasn't something that just "happened." There's little doubt that Michael Jordan was blessed with natural talent. If Michael hadn't dedicated himself to nurturing and developing that talent, he might still have become a very good ball-player, maybe even a star. But he would not have crossed that fine line that separates the good from the outstanding. In fact Michael Jordan may very well have crossed a line that no player before him has ever crossed.

Where does a person find the character and drive to become all he can be? In Michael Jordan's case, it's necessary to go back to the beginning, back to his parents—James and Delores Jordan—who had definite ideas about raising their family of five children.

When Michael was born on February 17, 1963, the family still lived in Brooklyn, one of the five boroughs of New York City. The Jordans were concerned about raising their family on the mean streets of Brooklyn, where drugs and violence could become a way of life for those unable to resist the temptations.

Rather than fight that battle, James and Delores Jordan decided to move the family to Wilmington, North Carolina. They felt the small-town, laid-back atmosphere of a sleepy southern seaport with a population of just 56,000 would be a better place to raise a family. So Wilmington was where Michael and his brothers and sisters grew up.

Once established in Wilmington, Mr. and Mrs. Jordan began to set an example for their children, exhibiting a willingness to work and achieve that never diminished. James Jordan began as a mechanic at a General Electric plant in Wilmington in 1967. Over the years, he worked up to dispatcher, then foreman, and finally to supervisor. Delores Jordan became a teller at the United Carolina Bank in Wilmington. She, too, was goal oriented and eventually became the head of customer relations at the bank's downtown branch.

"It was always that way in our family," James Jordan said. "We have always tried to make things happen rather than wait around for them to happen. And we've always found that if you work hard you can make it happen the way you want."

Of course, children don't learn those lessons overnight. Michael was more of a recreational athlete as a young boy, sometimes lazy, usually discouraged because he couldn't compete with his older brother, Larry. He wasn't very tall during his early years and didn't have much hope of being tall. There were no men in the Jordan family over six feet. So before he reached high school, he gave little thought to an athletic career, especially in basketball.

During his childhood, Michael was always close to his parents, as were the rest of the Jordan children. He would often play ball with his father or help him with projects in their garage workshop. The youngster couldn't help noticing that his father would always curl his tongue to the side of his mouth when he was concentrating intensely. Before long, Michael had picked up the habit and brought it with him into his sports activities.

Whether he was playing baseball, basketball, or football, Michael would shoot his tongue out during an intense moment or when he was concentrating the hardest. It was something he began doing automatically and a habit that would follow him onto the basketball court in high school, college, and the pros. Photos of the airborne Jordan almost always include the mouth open and the tongue jutting outward. Coaches would tell him his tongue could be badly cut if he were hit at the wrong time or tripped up. But Michael always refused to wear a mouthpiece or protective device. To him, this was simply another way to express his delight in the game, and he didn't want to curtail it.

"I remember my high school coach telling me I was going to bite my tongue off and find it on the floor or in my pocket," Michael said. "He even tried to get me to wear a mouthpiece when I played. But I just can't do it. I've tried to play with my mouth closed. But if my tongue's not out, I just can't play."

Baseball was the sport that Michael took to initially. At the age of 12 he was named the top player in his league and had his picture in the Wilmington *Morning Star*. He was extremely thin back then, but as a pitcher he could throw the ball hard. He also played the outfield.

By the time he reached D.C. Virgo Junior High School, Michael was a typical 15-year-old all-around athlete. He played three sports but wasn't really fanatical about any of them. Fred Lynch, who would be Michael's basketball coach at D.C. Virgo and his assistant coach later at Laney High, recalls meeting Michael for the first time.

"He liked to have a good time back then, but he also enjoyed playing sports," Coach Lynch said. "And he was good. Michael was a point guard in basketball and did a lot of scoring for us. He was also a quarterback in football, and a pitcher and outfielder with the baseball team. He did a little bit of everything, but two things stand out when I think back to that time.

"One was that Michael was very competitive. He hated losing, even then, and that made him work extremely hard when he played any of the sports. The other thing was that his parents were always very supportive of him. They attended all the games and always looked for something positive, whether Michael played well or the team played well."

By the time Michael reached Laney High School as a tenth grader, he was already 5'10", two inches taller than his father and three inches taller than his older brother, Larry. But no one really expected him to grow much more. He was also a good, but not great, basketball player, and there were absolutely no indications of an airborne future after Laney. In fact, Michael was really no more than a solid, young three-sport athlete with the potential to be a fine high school player in each sport.

Michael received his work ethic and strength of character from his parents, James and Delores Jordan. They all remained very close, even after Michael became a pro star. Here the family gathers in Chicago to celebrate Michael's twenty-sixth birthday, in 1989. The cake is in the shape of an Air Jordan basketball shoe. *(AP/Wide World Photo)*

Michael was the quarterback for the Laney JV football team in the fall. Shortly after that, he moved right into basketball and was the starting point guard on the JV squad. Then, near the end of the season, something happened that would have a great impact on young Michael, something that changed his thinking about basketball and may have been instrumental in starting him on the road to court stardom.

Michael felt he was putting together a good sophomore season, when the word filtered down that the varsity was going to bring up a JV player for the stretch run, which they hoped would include the state tournament. Young Michael held his breath. He wanted to be the one, wanted it very badly. But when word came down from varsity coach Clifton "Pop" Herring, it was Michael's teammate Leroy Smith who got the call.

"It was a tough thing for Michael to take," recalls Fred Lynch. "Even back then he had the kind of ego that drives all great players. But at that time we still didn't know just how good he was going to be. So there were really two reasons that Michael didn't get called: One was that we felt he would be better off remaining with the JVs and getting his minutes rather than sitting the bench with the varsity; the other was simple—Leroy Smith was about 6'5" and Michael was 5'10". What the varsity needed was height, a tall player. That made the choice relatively simple."

But that didn't make it any easier to accept. "I was disappointed," Michael admitted. "I was averaging over 20 points a game for the JVs, and with the state playoffs coming up, I thought I would get the call."

It got even worse than that. When the Laney team went to the regionals, Michael was allowed on the bus only because a student manager got sick. Once there, he didn't have a ticket to get in, so he had to carry the uniform of the team's best player, just as a manager would do. Then he had to sit on the bench, handing out towels during the game.

"I made up my mind right then and there that this would never happen to me again," Michael would say. "From that point on, I began working harder than ever on my basketball skills."

It was time to get serious.

CHAPTER 2

First Taste of Stardom

Michael's renewed dedication to basketball had one immediate drawback, however. He was so anxious to make the varsity as a junior that he began cutting classes to spend time practicing in the gym. Of course, no one can get away with cutting classes indefinitely, and it wasn't long before the teachers and administrators realized what was happening. Michael was warned, and when he did it one more time he was suspended. Yet he was so determined to become a better player that he continued to cut classes until he was suspended a third time. Then his father stepped in.

"When I asked Michael what his goal was, he told me he wanted to go to college," said James Jordan. "I told him there was no way it was going to happen, not the way he was going. He couldn't keep cutting classes and have any hope of going to college. I told him this in no uncertain terms, because I knew if I didn't do something about it right away, the situation was going to get worse."

The talk with his father brought Michael to his senses. "I knew he was right," Michael said. "I knew I had to concentrate more on my schoolwork if I wanted to reach my goal of going to college. I'd just have to find another way to get in my practice time on the court.

"Who knows what would have happened if my father hadn't talked to me. I was lucky enough to have parents who cared. They always gave me guidance and at the same time taught me to work hard."

Part of that work included one-on-one games with brother Larry at their backyard hoop. The two had been waging war behind their house for years, with Larry usually coming out on top. Even James Jordan noticed how his two sons went at it.

"I think Michael got so good because Larry used to beat him all the time," said Mr. Jordan. "He always took losing hard. He only began beating Larry once he started to really grow."

Even Michael remembers the games with Larry as something more than a friendly rivalry.

"My brother and I would play every day until my mom had to call us in," Michael said. "When we played we were opponents. We never thought of brotherhood at all. Sometimes, in fact, we would end up fighting."

But the hard-fought backyard games also helped. Larry Jordan was a fine ballplayer. When Michael grew taller than his brother, he started to win a few. Fred Lynch said he remembers Michael dunking the ball his sophomore year once in a while at practice, but never in a game. But Larry Jordan, at 5'7", could "dunk it any way you want it done." So Michael had a good teacher.

That wasn't the only thing that happened between Michael's sophomore and junior years at Laney. Out of nowhere, Michael suddenly shot up. When he returned to school in the fall, he had grown a full five inches, from 5'10" to 6'3". With no men in the Jordan family over six feet, Michael's unexpected growth spurt was hard to believe.

"It was almost as if he willed himself taller," James Jordan has said.

A taller Michael Jordan was simply a better version on the basketball court. Fred Lynch remembers the transformation well.

"Michael was always a slim, gangly kid, but no one ever thought he would get that tall," said the coach. "And for him it really worked out to be a blessing, because he always played guard, always handled the ball, and could shoot from the outside. Then, all of a sudden, he gets this 6'3" frame, and it just made him that much better. There was no clumsy stage, no time needed to adjust to his height. He was just a better basketball player, and he loved every minute of it."

Michael gave up football as a junior so he would have time to get ready for the basketball season. He played baseball for one more year, then dropped it as a senior so he could concentrate on postseason basketball all-star games. Finally he was down to concentrating on a single sport, something he said his mother wanted him to do all along.

As a junior he began a practice routine that would become a way of life. The teams would change, but

Michael's dedication to the sport and desire to become a better player would never diminish. Even though he was on the varsity, Michael showed up at JV practice, which was held from 5:30 to 7 P.M. He would do all the drills and even the killing wind sprints at the end. Then when the varsity took the floor from 7 to 9 P.M., Michael would practice with them all over again.

"Beginning his junior year, Michael was the hardest-working athlete I'd ever seen," said Fred Lynch. "He'd also be in the gym on Saturdays and Sundays, playing all day long. There may have been other kids with nearly as much talent as Michael, but they just didn't want to pay dues the way he did."

Michael's growing court success didn't translate into supreme self-confidence in other parts of his life. There were times early on when he was sensitive about his large ears and tended to stay away from the girls. Because he didn't know what the future would bring, he took a practical approach to life. In case he had to live alone, he made sure he studied home economics at Laney.

"I took home economics all three years," he said, "because I wanted to learn how to do things for myself. I learned to sew, to make outfits out of patterns. I remember making a shirt and a couple of pairs of pants. It wasn't always easy for me, but I did it."

What he often made look easy was the way he handled himself on the basketball court. All the hard work was beginning to pay off. He was becoming a star player, a kid who was a fierce competitor, and one who pushed his teammates, because more than anything else, he hated to lose.

"Michael was very coachable in high school," Fred Lynch recalls. "Like any high school player, if you let him get away with things, he would continue to do them. But he listened and did pretty much what we wanted him to do. One thing he always demanded was that the other players go as hard as he did. From that standpoint he was a pusher. It stemmed from his being so competitive and hating to lose. Michael was a sore loser.

"In fact he always felt he could have done better. Maybe that's what drove him to practice so hard. What he never did, though, was to blame his teammates if things didn't go well. He never came into the locker room after games and pointed fingers. That wasn't his style."

His style was to score in increasingly spectacular ways. Michael had his great leaping ability and was now beginning to use it on his twisting, turning drives to the hoop. He could also stick the jump shot. Along with an increasing variety of offensive moves, he was also developing the ability to play even harder in tough situations. When the game was on the line at crunch time, Michael Jordan wanted the basketball.

Not every player wants the ball in his hands when the outcome is at stake. The great ones do, and the very great ones have the ability to deliver the goods more often than not. It's a quality that can't be taught. It usually emerges as the young athlete grows and matures. That's what was happening with Michael during his junior year at Laney High School. And never was it more in evidence than in a holiday tournament game against New Hanover that year.

New Hanover was another Wilmington high school, and when the town rivals met for the championship, the intensity level couldn't have been higher. The game was a real battle, with the New Hanover team having the lead in the closing minutes. That was when Michael Jordan took over. Suddenly he was on fire. His teammates got him the ball, and he went to work. He began scoring on everything—drives, jump shots, free throws. Finally it came down to the last second, and it was Michael again, hitting a clutch jump shot to give Laney the victory.

Incredibly, Michael had scored the final 15 Laney points, taking the game over and winning it for his team. It was a high school version of *showtime,* and those who saw his virtuoso performance will never forget it.

"There were a lot of games he simply controlled like that," recalls Fred Lynch. "In fact, we saw quite of bit of it his junior year. If a team was playing us man to man, Michael felt as if he was going to score, and no one could stop him. When he got on a roll like that, the other players knew what they had to do. If he didn't already have the ball—which he often did— they would get it to him. Everyone had the same objective—winning the game."

Michael was beginning to make a name for himself. There was a Wilmington school official named Mike Brown, who had graduated from the University of North Carolina. Carolina grads are always looking out for the basketball program, and when Brown saw Jordan play against New Hanover, he contacted his alma mater and told them there was a player at Laney they should look at. Coach Dean Smith dispatched one of his assistants, Bill Guthridge, to Wilmington to check out a thin youngster who could explode offensively at any time.

"My feeling was that Michael had the potential and ability to be an Atlantic Coast Conference player," says Guthridge, thinking back some dozen or so years. "You knew he was going to be good, but you didn't know how good. And you certainly couldn't see greatness in him at the time."

So the first reaction was only a "maybe." But remember, North Carolina is traditionally one of the finest collegiate teams in the country, and Coach Dean Smith recruits only top players. One thing was certain, though: The university rarely overlooked any of the top ballplayers from its own state.

At that point, however, Michael wasn't thinking much about North Carolina, either. While he was growing up in the mid-1970s, he had always favored North Carolina State, which had a team that won the National Championship in 1974. N.C. State had a 6'4" superstar named David Thompson, who was, in effect, an earlier version of Michael Jordan. Thompson was a skywalker who at times seemed to defy gravity. It's no wonder he was Michael's first real idol. But despite his rapid growth and increasing success as a Laney junior, Michael had no delusions of grandeur about his future.

"I never thought I'd be able to play at a Division I school," he said. "In fact, nobody from my high school had ever played Division I. I guess that's why it really shocked me when North Carolina began recruiting me. I never thought that would happen."

But it didn't happen until after the basketball season had ended. Even then, it needed a special event, an extra push, something that would elevate Michael to a class labeled "top college prospects." Though Michael had a fine junior season at Laney,

17

Michael's coach felt he needed tougher competition. So Clifton Herring began writing letters to Howie Garfinkel, who ran the Five-Star Basketball Camp during the summer months. Five-Star was the place where many of the best high school prospects gathered to show their stuff and to learn.

Coach Herring soon had some support. Roy Williams, who was a part-time assistant coach at North Carolina then (and would later become the head coach at Kansas), went to speak to Tom Konchalski, a high school talent evaluator who was associated with the camp. Of Jordan, Williams said, "We don't know how good he is, but he could become a great player."

The campaign worked. Michael was given a job as a waiter at the camp and told he had been accepted for one week. As it turned out, that was all the time he needed. Air Jordan, budding superstar, was about to be born.

Playing against some of the country's best high schoolers, most of whom would be recruited by Division I schools, Michael not only excelled, he dominated. His ball handling, speed, moves, and leaping ability were too much for the others. Tom Konchalski, who helped secure Michael's invitation, joined the others and looked twice at this kid from Wilmington.

"The first time he took a jump shot he got up so high it was like there was no defender," Konchalski said. "It was like he was playing a different game."

During the week, Michael excelled at every phase of the sport. When it ended, he had won five trophies for individual excellence and was invited to remain for a second week. It was more of the same. All the work, all the hours of practice, all the games with his brother in the backyard, all the crunch-time shots for Laney—the results poured forth at Five-Star. In the second week, Michael won four more trophies, easily setting a record for the most trophies taken by an individual.

"I wasn't there," said Fred Lynch, "but I spoke with several coaches who were, and they were all amazed at how outstanding Michael was. To a man, they said he was just heads better than anyone else. In two weeks everyone knew he was a ballplayer. He came out of the camp rated the top high school player at that time.

"It's funny, but coaching at a small high school, you never get a chance to see a whole lot of kids. You only hear about how good certain players are. So when we first read, then heard, how well Michael had done, we were all amazed."

So was Michael. His experience at Five-Star told him he could play with the big boys, and many of his previous doubts were erased.

"Nobody knew me till I went up there, and I was scared," he would say later. "But I played my best ever at the camp and really got some recognition."

He would continue to work and practice, his goal of attending college and playing ball now more of a reality. In fact, remembering his Five-Star experience, Michael says, "It was the turning point of my life."

Despite his new reputation, there wasn't a mad rush from colleges around the country to recruit him. Most of the action came from within, and around, the state—North Carolina, South Carolina, North Carolina State, and Maryland. Though N.C. State had been his favorite when the great David Thompson played there, Michael eliminated the Wolfpack early. South Carolina, usually not a national power, made a strong bid for him, as did the University of Maryland. Fred Lynch says that at one point he was real close to going to South Carolina.

"But then he took a trip to the North Carolina campus, and that was it."

It wasn't the usual recruiting trip, where a prospective athlete can be wined and dined and wooed. Michael went to the campus at Chapel Hill as part of a minority student program known as Project Uplift. So his first visit to the school was as a student, not a ballplayer.

"The coaches didn't even know I was there," he said. "It gave me a chance to look at the place as a prospective student would."

So Michael signed to attend the University of North Carolina even before his senior season at Laney High began. Fred Lynch described why Michael wasn't recruited by more schools and also explained how things could have been different if a certain school had shown interest in him.

"First, there is the Carolina mystique," Lynch explains. "I think a lot of schools from other parts of the country just shy away from North Carolina kids because they figure Dean Smith is going to get the best players for Carolina. So there weren't very many out-of-state schools after him and none from the West Coast."

That fact once prompted Michael to say an interesting thing to Fred Lynch.

"Michael told me that if UCLA had recruited him, he would have gone out there. All they had to do was come here to look at him and invite him to the coast. He said he would have gone. Fortunately, for a lot of folks around here, they didn't, and he didn't."

When Michael Jordan was a youngster, his family was always very close. It's the same way now as his son, Jeffrey, and his wife, Juanita, help Michael celebrate his greatest moment, an NBA Championship. The celebration was held on June 14, 1991, at Grant Park in downtown Chicago. *(AP/Wide World Photo)*

In one sense, Michael could now relax. His immediate future was set. He would be receiving a basketball scholarship to the University of North Carolina, beginning in the autumn of 1981. His immediate goal had been reached. As Fred Lynch remembers, Michael began preparing for Carolina and wasn't worrying about anything beyond that.

"Michael always took things one step at a time," said Coach Lynch. "He didn't talk about playing pro ball, only doing well at Carolina. It wasn't until a couple of years later, when he realized that pro ball could become a reality, that he began talking about the NBA as his next goal."

There was no way Michael was going to rest on his laurels. His hard work and practice routine only intensified when he was a senior. Every day, Coach Herring would come by his house and pick Michael up before sunrise. By about 6 A.M. Michael was working out in the Laney gym, practicing his moves, his ball handling, and shooting. It was an intense workout, even before the school day began. For a high school kid, that took a lot of discipline.

Michael had grown more. He was now approaching 6'5" and was one of the country's dominant high school players. Though the future was set, he didn't loaf through his final season at Laney. He still worked hard, pushed his teammates to excel, and took over the game at crunch time because he still hated to lose. He averaged 27.8 points and 12 rebounds a game. Pretty good, especially considering that high school games are just 32 minutes long.

By his senior year Michael was spending more time in the air, flying toward the hoop from every conceivable angle, mouth open and tongue hanging out. At

6'5", there was one thing he could do much better than he could as a 5'10" sophomore.

"I saw Michael dunk once at practice when he was a sophomore," said Fred Lynch, "but never in a game. By the time he was a senior, that had changed. Not only would he dunk in a game, but now it was any way you wanted it done. He could really put on a show."

Michael Jordan graduated from Laney High School in June of 1981. His friends from Wilmington still called him Mike and treated him as they always had, as a friend, not a celebrity or a star. His parents, according to Fred Lynch and others, never allowed him to think he was great or better than anyone. Their influence always helped to keep him on an even keel.

Now it was on to a new life at Chapel Hill, North Carolina, where he would concentrate on books and Coach Dean Smith's Tar Heels. Despite his success at Laney and the Five-Star camp, Michael Jordan still had doubts, still wondered if he could crack the big time. It wouldn't be long before Michael and the rest of the basketball world found out.

PART

TWO

PART

TWO

CHAPTER 3

The Shot

Michael went to North Carolina in the fall of 1981. He knew he was there to study and to play big-time college hoops. He was determined to do his best both with the books and basketball.

It was no secret that the North Carolina program and the current team were among the best in the country. Coach Smith and the Tar Heels had made it to the NCAA finals in 1977. They had a powerful team that year, led by a trio of All-Americans—Walter Davis, Mike O'Koren, and Phil Ford—yet were upset by Marquette, 67–59.

Four years later, as Michael Jordan was wrapping up his Laney High career and anticipating his move to Chapel Hill, the Tar Heels were once again making noise in the NCAA. As was the case in 1977, this North Carolina team featured a trio of All-American-caliber players—Al Wood, James Worthy, and Sam Perkins. Yet for the second time in four years, Carolina was beaten in the finals, this time 63–50 by Bobby Knight's Indiana Hoosiers. The team finished at 29-8.

Though Wood had graduated, both Worthy and Perkins were back, as were Jimmy Black and Matt Doherty, two more solid players. Those four supposedly had a lock on starting jobs. Only the second guard slot was up for grabs. Yet few thought that a freshman kid named Jordan would have a real shot. Even Michael was skeptical.

Before practice officially began, Michael played continually, working as hard as ever. One day he went over to the gym and suddenly found himself in a pickup game with some very heavy dudes. The graduated Al Wood was there, working out before going to his first NBA camp. Then there was Mitch Kupchak, another Tar Heel alumnus who had already had some fine years in the NBA and was still active. James Worthy was there too. He was expected to be the star of the 1981–82 squad.

"I was so nervous, my hands were sweating," Michael remembered. "I saw all these All-Americans, and I thought I was just the lowest thing on the totem pole."

Then the game began. Michael worked his way into the flow slowly, feeling out the situation. It may have been just a pickup game, but all these guys were competitors, and the longer they played, the more intense they became, the more heated the action became. Finally, it came down to crunch time and, as usual, the real Michael Jordan emerged. He remembered it this way.

"Al Wood was guarding me, and it was tied—next

basket wins," he said. "I had the ball. I was nervous, because people were watching, and I still wasn't sure I belonged out there. I went baseline and Wood went with me. When I made my move, Geoff Compton, a seven-footer, came over to help out. I went up with the ball and thought I was trapped. But I just kept going up, wound up going over both of them, and dunked. When I came down to the floor I said to myself, 'Was that really me?'"

Once practice began Michael quickly showed that he fit in. Assistant coach Bill Guthridge remembers how Michael was at the outset of his freshman year.

"He was eager to learn and eager to do what we wanted him to do," Guthridge said. "Plus, he was an excellent athlete. He was also confident that he could play, but not cocky. In fact, he was never cocky during all his time here. He always listened and worked hard at practice, did what he was supposed to do, and blended in very well with the vets. They accepted him for his ability and his personality."

There was little doubt that Michael was in the running for a starting slot. That possibility seemed to fade somewhat when he missed two weeks of practice because of a broken blood vessel in his ankle. But once back on the court, he continued to excel. Some felt he wouldn't start because he was a freshman, because Coach Smith preferred going with veterans. Since freshmen had become eligible for varsity play, only three first-year players—Phil Ford, Mike O'Koren, and James Worthy—had become Tar Heel starters. All three were exceptional.

Would Michael make it four? Bill Guthridge said that the door was open. "It's a misconception that North Carolina doesn't start freshmen," Guthridge said. "If everything is equal, Coach Smith will start the older player. But he wants to have his best team out there, no matter what the class of the players. That means everyone, including the freshmen, has six weeks of practice to earn a spot on the team."

With the opener against Kansas fast approaching, four of the starting spots were definitely filled. Sophomore Matt Doherty would move in at forward with the two returning stars, junior forward Worthy and sophomore center Perkins. Senior Jimmy Black would be the point guard. Returners Jim Braddock and Dean Shaffer were two possibilities at off guard. Then there were three freshmen—Buzz Peterson, Lynwood Robinson, and Michael. Coach Smith took it down to the wire. He didn't announce the fifth starter until he posted the lineup on the bulletin board before the game.

"I didn't know I'd be starting until I saw my name on the board," Michael said. "And believe me, I was nervous."

There were some 11,666 fans on hand for the opener, and the game was being shown on regional television as well. No wonder Michael had the jitters. He had come a long way from his sophomore year at Laney, when he still had trouble beating his brother in the backyard and was forced to carry another player's uniform so he could go to the playoffs.

Now he was in the starting lineup for the North Carolina Tar Heels, a preseason top-ten pick and a team considered one of the finest in the country. The opener with Kansas wouldn't be easy. A year earlier, the Jayhawks had beaten the Tar Heels by a single point and also had a fine returning squad. This time

After a fine high school career and outstanding performance at the Five Star Basketball Camp, a youthful Michael Jordan began his career at the University of North Carolina, where his game-winning shot at the end of his freshman year gave the Tar Heels a National Championship. *(Courtesy University of North Carolina)*

the game was on a neutral court and would be a good test.

The first time Michael came down the court and had the ball, he thought, "I don't know if I should shoot it or not." So his first shot, a medium-range jumper, was off the mark. But less than a minute later he got another chance and this time connected on a baseline jumper over a pair of Kansas players. It was Carolina's first two points of the game, and he made it look easy.

But it wasn't an easy game for North Carolina. The Tar Heels held the lead most of the way, though they couldn't break it open. Michael had to keep playing at a high level. When it ended, the Tar Heels had a 74–67 victory with a solid team effort. Michael had played 31 minutes, hit 5 of 10 shots from the field and 2 of 2 from the free throw line, for 12 points. After the game he seemed relieved that it was over and that it had gone so well.

"Jimmy [Black] told me last night not to be nervous, not to worry about the crowd or the TV cameras," Michael said. "Then, as the game went along, I began to get more into the flow. Once it was over, I realized I was just as good as anybody else."

Backcourt partner Black, who had to work the closest with Michael, said something which would later become one of the great understatements in Tar Heel history. "Mike's a good player," said Black. "Good players don't get nervous in games."

Michael had certainly been good in his collegiate debut, good enough so that Coach Smith didn't consider replacing him in the starting lineup. He was in until his play dictated otherwise. He had another 12 points in a 73–62 win over Southern California, only this time he accomplished it with some deadly 6-for-8 shooting. Then the team returned home to Carmichael Auditorium to play Tulsa.

In this one, Michael really began to give everyone a glimpse of things to come. He played just 22 minutes, but it definitely came under the category of quality time. He had hit on 11 of 15 shots from the floor to crack the 20-point mark for the first time. He also added five rebounds and three assists as the Tar Heels remained unbeaten with a 78–70 victory. After just three games there was little doubt that the thin freshman from Wilmington was making a major contribution to the team.

It was reflected in the results, as North Carolina continued to win, rolling over Florida, Rutgers, Kentucky, Penn State, Santa Clara, William & Mary, and Maryland. The Tar Heels were 10-0 by the end of the first week in January and were ranked as the number-one team in the country. Worthy was playing especially well and seemed like a sure shot to be a consensus All-American. The 6'9" Perkins wasn't a huge center but could usually hold his own against much bigger men. Doherty had become a solid forward and good shooter, while Jimmy Black was a very competent point guard. Add the explosiveness of the freshman Jordan, and Dean Smith had quite a formidable starting unit.

Now the entire team would be put to the test. The Tar Heels had a January 9 showdown with the number-two team in the country, ACC rival Virginia, a club led by 7'4" center Ralph Sampson. Sampson was a talented big man who could dominate a game, but he was also a guy who would sometimes disappear from the offense and defense while still on the court. But in this contest against the Tar Heels, Sampson was there, on his game, and tough to stop.

North Carolina had to play team basketball to counteract this quick-moving, slick-shooting giant. While Virginia led most of the way, the Tar Heels hung close. It was 54–53, Virginia, with four minutes left. Then a Sampson dunk gave the Cavaliers a 58–57 advantage as the clock approached the two-minute mark. But the Tar Heels regained the lead and upped it to 61–58 on two free throws by Jim Braddock. The final score was 65–60, as North Carolina remained unbeaten.

Once again it was a team effort, a trademark of Dean Smith ballclubs. Michael didn't have to dominate to contribute. After a relatively quiet first half, he hit 5 of 7 second-half shots to finish with 16 points, playing a big part in the victory.

There was no prima donna in the lanky freshman. Assistant coach Bill Guthridge was impressed with the way Michael listened to the coaching staff and kept working.

"Michael was always a great listener, always listened to what Coach Smith had to say," Guthridge recalls. "In fact, he was one of the best ever at paying attention and then working on the things we talked about. That was one reason he kept getting better and better."

Coach Smith was impressed with the fact that while Michael was just a freshman and inexperienced in the pressures of big-time ball, he rarely took a bad shot or forced a shot. He had blended in with the veterans and become an integral part of the ballclub. One writer remarked that Michael's talents were rare in that he was able to fit within the N.C. system and still was able to let loose with one of his great moves at just the right time. In other words, he had gained respect.

Both Michael and the team continued to play well for the rest of the season. The Tar Heels wound up ACC regular season champs, with just two losses overall. Michael finished his first year with a 13.5 scoring average for 34 games (including the NCAA tournament)—far from the Air Jordan numbers of today, but for a college freshman starting for a ballclub that emphasized the team concept, he had done exceptionally well. He shot 53.4 percent from the field and made 72.2 percent of his free throws. In addition, he grabbed 149 rebounds and had 61 assists and 41 steals. For his effort, he was named Atlantic Coast Conference Rookie of the Year.

Of course, a successful regular season is just a prelude to the postseason. Every team's goal is the NCAA tournament, the Final Four, and a national championship. North Carolina had won the title once, back in 1957, when the Tar Heels defeated Wilt Chamberlain and Kansas in a classic triple-overtime ballgame. But Dean Smith wasn't the coach then, Frank McGuire was. Smith, however, had taken his Tar Heel teams to the Final Four six times. On three occasions—1968, 1977, and 1981—he had reached the championship game, only to come up short. So the veteran coach hoped his 1982 club could bring him his first national title.

Before they could worry about the Final Four, the Tar Heels had to compete in the postseason ACC tournament, the results to determine site and seedings in the larger NCAA tourney. Once again, it came down to North Carolina and Virginia in the tournament final. And once again the two teams slugged away at each other in a close, hard-fought ballgame. Late in the game, Virginia had a three-point lead, and with big Ralph Sampson in the middle, it was beginning to look pretty safe.

But it was the freshman who suddenly took charge of the game. Michael got hot and hit four straight jump shots, erasing the Cavalier lead and propelling the Tar Heels to a 47–45 victory and the ACC tournament title. Michael had scored only 10 points, but eight of them came in the closing minutes to insure the victory. For his efforts, he was named to the all-tournament team. The victory made North Carolina the top seed in the Eastern Regional and also in the entire NCAA tournament. Would this club be able to do what other fine Tar Heel teams couldn't and bring Dean Smith that elusive national championship?

At the outset of the tournament, North Carolina was definitely a favorite. But suddenly, the Tar Heels weren't playing very well. They had one scare, then another, as they battled to reach the Final Four. The first came from tiny James Madison of Virginia, a team that had already upset Ohio State. Against the Tar Heels, James Madison was formidable once again. North Carolina had just a 31–29 lead at the half, and it didn't get any better after intermission. Despite the presence of Worthy, Perkins, and Jordan, North Carolina barely escaped with a 52–50 victory.

It wasn't exactly a warning to other teams that would face the top seed. The Tar Heels had to regroup. But in the regional semifinals at Raleigh, North Carolina, the Crimson Tide of Alabama played one of their best games of the year. They pressed the Tar Heels to the final minutes before North Carolina prevailed, 74–69. It was another close one, but the great teams always manage to win the close ones. When the Tar Heels topped Villanova by 10, they were regional champs and headed for the Final Four, which was being held at the Superdome in New Orleans.

Along with the Tar Heels, the other three teams vying for the title were the University of Houston, which won the Midwest Regional; Louisville, which took the Mideast Regional; and Georgetown, winners with ease in the West Region.

It was the Tar Heels against the Cougars of Houston in one semifinal. While the game wasn't a blowout, it was probably North Carolina's best team effort of the tourney. Perkins was outstanding, with 25 points and 10 rebounds, while the Carolina defense held Houston high-scorer Rob Williams without a field goal. Carolina won the game, 68–63, and was in the finals.

The Tar Heels' opponent would be Georgetown. The Hoyas had beaten Louisville in a defensive struggle, 50–46, in the other semifinal to set up a great matchup for the title. Georgetown coach John Thompson was building a great team. He had an All-American guard in Eric "Sleepy" Floyd and a host of hustling defensive-minded players. Add to that a seven-foot freshman center named Patrick Ewing, who was strong and intimidating, and Georgetown certainly had the firepower to win the national title. The Hoyas came into the title game with a 30-6 record and seemed to be peaking at the perfect time.

With 61,612 fans jammed into the Superdome, the game started strangely. The first four North Carolina shots never reached the basket. Patrick Ewing swatted them all away, only the refs ruled he got each on its downward trajectory. That meant it was goal tending, an illegal maneuver. The baskets counted. The Tar Heels had scored eight points without the ball going through the hoop.

Maybe Ewing was trying to give North Carolina a message, trying to intimidate them. But it didn't work. Despite the presence of the big man in the middle, North Carolina continued to play its game. So did Georgetown, and the contest became a brutal battle. Each basket came grudgingly. Neither team could pull away.

Worthy was the Tar Heel star in the first half, scoring 18 points in a fine performance. The problem was, he wasn't getting that much help, the swarming Georgetown defense shutting down players such as Doherty and Black. Perkins had to concentrate on defense. Though Michael was playing a fine game, he hadn't had many scoring chances. At the half, Georgetown held a 32–31 lead. It could have been even worse, because at one point the Hoyas led by as many as six.

In the second half the battle continued. As had been his pattern, Michael began picking up the pace. Not only was he beginning to score, but the thin freshman was doing a great job on the boards, challenging Ewing and the other Hoya forwards for the ball. Still neither team managed to break the game open. Only a few points separated the two clubs during the final 20 minutes. The tension mounted.

With six minutes left in the game, Worthy hit a pair of free throws that gave Carolina the lead, 57–56. Georgetown missed its next shot, and when the Tar Heels got the ball, Coach Smith ordered them into their famed four-corner offense. That was a spread formation designed to hold the ball and slow the pace of the game. Smith would use it for minutes on end before the 45-second clock was introduced to the college game.

The pace remained slow. With about 3:30 left, the Tar Heels had a 59–58 lead. Michael then made a beautiful driving shot over Ewing's defense to raise the score, 61–58. But the Georgetown center answered with a jump shot at the 2:37 mark to cut the Carolina lead to a single point at 61–60. Carolina tried to work for a good shot. Georgetown's Eric Smith fouled Matt Doherty, who missed his free throw with just 1:19 left.

Georgetown went on offense, working the ball carefully and looking for a chance to go inside to Ewing. But the Carolina defense kept collapsing around the big guy. Finally, with just 32 seconds left, Sleepy Floyd hit a 12-foot clutch jumper to give the Hoyas a 62–61 lead. There could be no four-corner offense now. Carolina needed a basket quickly. During a timeout, Coach Thompson told his team to watch Worthy, who already had 28 points on 13-for-17 shooting from the floor. Michael was the second-highest Carolina scorer, having hit 6 of 12 with two free throws, for 14 points. But Worthy would seem to be the man.

The Tar Heels knew enough not to rush or take a bad shot. They patiently worked the ball around. Sure enough, the Hoya defense watched Worthy closely. Matt Doherty had the ball, and he suddenly whipped a pass to Michael, who was on the left baseline, 16 feet from the hoop. With 17 seconds left on the clock, Michael did what he had done so often at Laney

High—he went up for a jump shot with the game on the line.

"I had a good feeling about it when I let it go," he would say later, "but I didn't know for sure."

A split second later the 61,000-plus fans and millions more on television all knew.

SWISH!

The shot dropped through the hoop without touching the rim. The crowd erupted. Michael's clutch shot had given Carolina the lead, 63–62. The Hoyas still had a chance. Georgetown guard Fred Brown brought the ball downcourt. He thought he spotted Sleepy Floyd to his left and without looking flipped him the ball. Only, it wasn't Floyd. It was James Worthy, who was as surprised as everyone else when the ball came to him. Worthy just reversed direction, but was fouled.

Though he missed both free throws, there were now only two seconds left. Georgetown couldn't get a good shot off. The Tar Heels had won it. And it had been Michael's clutch shot that did the trick and had given Dean Smith his first national championship.

Worthy's 28 points would earn him the game's MVP prize. But Michael had also been brilliant. He not only scored 16 big points, but led the Tar Heels with 9 rebounds, second in the entire game to Ewing's 11. His play had earned him a spot on the all-tournament team, the only freshman to achieve that honor.

He had also assured himself a place in North Carolina's glorious basketball history. Though Michael was only a freshman, his feat put him right up there with all the other Carolina greats. In addition, the picture of his clutch hoop would forever be

With his tongue characteristically protruding from his mouth, Michael operates against Clemson during the Atlantic Coast Conference Championships in 1983. As a Tar Heel, Michael was a hero as a freshman and Player of the Year the next two seasons. *(AP/Wide World Photo)*

remembered for bringing his school the national crown. From that point on, every Carolina alumnus, every student who was there, and all those to follow would know exactly what was meant whenever someone mentioned—

The shot!

CHAPTER 4

Player of the Year

It goes without saying that Michael Jordan was an instant celebrity, both in North Carolina and nationally. The national hoopla lasted just a few days, but Michael showed he could handle himself well under pressure of another kind—the media crunch. He was still a student, however, and had to get back to Chapel Hill to finish his classes for the year. Once back on campus, Michael found that he couldn't escape being a hero.

"I've got a lot more friends now than I used to have," Michael said, referring to his newfound celebrity. "People come up to me now and say they knew me when I was small. I don't know them, but they seem to know me.

"But I'm the same person I always was. I try to write and call and stay in touch with all the people I knew before. I don't ever want to change."

One of those old friends was high school coach Clifton Herring. Michael told the story of a prediction made by his former coach.

"Coach Herring predicted we would win the national championship in my freshman year," Michael related. "He also predicted I would play a major part in the victory. I called him after the game, and he went berserk."

Never one to rest on his laurels where basketball was concerned, Michael took less than a week off from his sport after the NCAA tourney ended. The title game was on a Monday. Six days later Michael was bored and wanting some action.

"It was a Sunday, and I didn't have anything to do," he said. "So I came over to Carmichael Auditorium, and there was a lot of good competition out there. So I decided to play. From then on, I came back every day. It was like I was addicted to the game. I tried to stay away, but I couldn't."

But basketball wasn't the only thing on Michael's agenda at Chapel Hill. He did have a life away from the court. In the classroom he was a solid B student who had chosen geography as his major field of study. No easy courses for him. He was serious about his studies from the day he walked onto the campus. Despite the rigors of big-time college basketball, Michael balanced his time, and while he couldn't always carry a full course load, he never looked for shortcuts when it came to academics.

Michael's roommate on campus from his freshman year was Buzz Peterson, a reserve guard on the Carolina team. The two had met at the Five-Star camp and forged a friendship that carried over to Carolina. The fact that a black and a white could live in racial harmony was a fine example for everyone. The relationship between the two friends and ball-players was special.

"We met at the Five-Star camp and then came to Carolina together," Peterson said. "What impressed me about Michael was his love for his parents and his family. He was also a fun guy to be around, except when he was on the basketball court. Then he became deadly serious."

Michael's father also talked about the relationship between the two friends, who spent a great deal of time at each other's homes.

"It's really a beautiful friendship," said James Jordan. "From the first time we met Buzz's parents at the camp we hit it off. They're likable and easy to know. We've always looked at Michael's friends as our sons, and we advise them as we do Michael.

"When Buzz hurt a knee, Michael and all his teammates hurt for him. That's the way it is with the Carolina team. They're close."

The two youngsters also played pool, golf, cards, and even Monopoly together. Peterson attests to Michael's strong desire to win—in everything.

"There were times when Michael made me stay up all night playing cards or pool, refusing to go to sleep until he was winning again," Peterson said.

The well-matched roommates also agreed to limit their social activities during the basketball season.

"It was just classes, studying, and basketball," said Peterson. "We didn't want any distractions."

Michael continued to play and work at his game during the remainder of the school year and in the summer months.

He joined a college all-star team for a summer overseas tour and played in some rough games against foreign players who were professionals in their own lands.

"I got a chance to see what pro ball was like," Michael said, "and I really felt out of place. I had never played that rough before."

It was all a learning experience. Back at Chapel Hill in the fall of 1982, Michael found that The Shot was still very much with him. It was something no one around the campus would let him forget. For openers, the 1982 Chapel Hill–Carrboro telephone directory had a photograph of him taking the crucial jumper. A restaurant near the North Carolina campus, aptly named the Four Corners, had a sandwich named for him. The Jordan consisted of crab salad on pita with lettuce and tomato.

"I enjoyed the public recognition at first," Michael admitted. "Three years earlier I never dreamed a kid would ever ask me for an autograph. But sometimes all the recognition isn't easy to handle. When I'm noticed in a restaurant it can be embarrassing. That's when I get the feeling that basketball just follows me the entire day."

Michael knew that there couldn't be any distractions as he prepared for his sophomore season. James Worthy had decided to forego his senior year at Carolina to become eligible for the NBA draft. Without the All-American forward, an even larger burden would be placed on the shoulders of Michael Jordan, who had even grown some more. He now stood 6'6" and weighed close to 200 pounds.

"It was obvious as soon as we started practice that

Michael had been working very hard in the off-season," said assistant coach Bill Guthridge. "Even though he had made the winning shot against George-town, it was obvious that he was a better all-around shooter as a sophomore. He had also improved defensively. In fact, he improved tremendously. We give out a weekly defensive award, and Michael didn't win it once as a freshman. He would win it 12 times during his sophomore year. We all knew right away he wasn't the kind of kid to rest on his laurels."

Michael's work ethic was well known, and after The Shot he felt he had more reason to improve on an already impressive product.

"I couldn't be just Michael Jordan anymore," he said. "I was now Michael Jordan, who made the winning shot against Georgetown. But I didn't want to be remembered only for that. I wanted to be recognized as a complete player, a guy who just doesn't come through the last minute, but one who's there the entire game."

According to Bill Guthridge, Michael was well on the way to doing that.

"Michael was an excellent athlete when he came here," the coach said, "but he became an even better athlete each year. For example, we always had the players run the 40-yard dash each year. Michael wasn't the fastest guy, and as a freshman he and his roommate, Buzz Peterson, were about even. But the next year he beat Buzz pretty badly. I think it was because he grew and matured physically later than others. Most players who come into the program are as tall as they're gonna get by the time they arrive here."

Two things were obvious once the 1982–83 season began. Without Worthy, the Tar Heels weren't the same 32-2 team they had been the year before. But they were still a solid ballclub, especially with Michael Jordan in the lineup. In fact, it was apparent early in the year that Michael was playing at a much higher level as a sophomore. He began putting together a string of performances that could have made up an impressive highlight film.

Against Duke he threw in a career-best 32 points "with what seemed like relatively little effort," as one newspaper put it. He later topped that with a 39-point performance against Georgia Tech. Against Virginia, Michael sparked an 11-point Tar Heel rally in the final four minutes of a 64–63 victory over Ralph Sampson and company.

In that game Michael scored the final four points on a tip-in of a teammate's shot, followed by a steal and dunk. He then grabbed the rebound off a final Cavalier shot, getting to the ball before Sampson. Against Tulane, Michael stole the ball and hit a last-second jumper to tie the game, which the Tar Heels finally won in triple overtime.

Then in a game against arch rival Maryland, Michael came from nowhere to block a last-second layup and preserve a 72–71 North Carolina victory. There was little doubt about his abilities now. He was a superstar performer, one of the best in the country. When he popped for another 32 in a return match with Duke, the Blue Devils' All-American guard, Johnny Dawkins, said:

"Jordan goes all out. Not just physically, like he used to, but now he outthinks you on both offense and defense. Of all the players, he's the most impressive."

There were more testimonials as the year went on. Bruce Dalrymple of Georgia Tech called him "an incredible worker with an incredible amount of talent. His attitude is, you can push me or hit me, but I'm going to do what has to be done. It shows on his face, and that's what makes Jordan so great."

But perhaps the most telling comment was made by Tom Newell, an NBA scout for the Golden State Warriors.

"There is one phenomenon in college ball," Newell said, "and his name is Michael Jordan."

So the pros were already watching—and waiting. But Michael still had not given any indication of coming out early. His former teammate James Worthy had already said that Michael "will be a star the instant he steps into the NBA. There's no question that he'll be great."

Michael's quick retort was, "I'm not thinking about that now."

He continued to work hard as Carolina won another ACC title. This time, however, without as much firepower, they lost to Georgia, 82–77, in the NCAA regionals, a game in which Michael scored 26 points. The 32-2 national champs of a year earlier finished the 1982–83 season at a respectable 28-8.

At season's end all Michael's numbers were up. He scored 721 points, for an average of 20 per game. He hit on 53.5 percent of his shots from the field and 73.6 from the foul line. He also averaged 5.5 rebounds a game and had 56 assists and 78 steals. Needless to say, he was a consensus All-American. That was honor enough. But shortly afterward, he was selected for the ultimate honor, that of College Basketball's Player of the Year. It almost seemed as if there were no more worlds for him to conquer as a collegian.

Yet the day after the Tar Heels' NCAA elimination by Georgia, Michael was back in the gym, going through a long shooting and practicing session, telling anyone who would listen that he "couldn't wait for the next game."

There was plenty of basketball during the off-season, everything from pickup games to a starring role with the United States team at the Pan American Games. Michael was the leading scorer as the U.S. won a gold medal. Yet with all his dazzling success, Michael remained levelheaded, the same hardworking student-athlete who had come to Carolina two years earlier. Though he easily could have fallen into the trap of being the idolized, pampered athlete open to all temptations, he managed to avoid these problems completely. Once again the strength of his family and support group was cited as the reason.

"My parents warned me about the traps," Michael would say on more than one occasion. "The drugs and drinks, the streets that could catch you if you got careless. I was lazy about some things. I never got into mowing the lawn or doing hard jobs, but I wasn't careless."

Assistant coach Bill Guthridge put it even more succinctly when asked how Michael avoided the pits into which so many fine athletes had fallen.

"He's just a tremendous person who comes from a great family," said Guthridge.

After two years at the University of North Carolina, Michael Jordan seemed to have it all.

CHAPTER 5

A Difficult Decision

Even though Michael's achievements were considerable, he was still under tremendous pressure. It never seemed to stop. All-American Sam Perkins was also back for the 1983–84 season, along with two other starters and three strong candidates for the point guard spot. Yet Michael felt he would have to be a more dominant performer in order for the Tar Heels to be successful again. There wasn't really a need for him to feel that way. Even the cautious Dean Smith acknowledged that his bench was the deepest it had been in a long time.

"We have a chance to be very good this year," the veteran coach said. Despite this, Michael was doing something that was, in a way, uncharacteristic of him. He was putting a great deal of pressure on himself.

"After my freshman year, when we won the

NCAAs, I figured that was the way it was supposed to be," he admitted. "Everyone else was going crazy, and I was just acting normal. I didn't realize the full impact of what we had done or how special it was. I was still a little boy in a man's body. But when we lost [the next year], I realized how much winning meant and also how hard I had to work and how hard the team had to work."

The result was the first real slump of Michael Jordan's career, a prolonged period when he seemed to lose the edge. The first four games of the season saw him averaging just 14 points, with a total of 11 rebounds. That wasn't Michael. Fortunately, the other players were picking up the slack, and the team was winning. When he scored 19 against Syracuse and 25 against Dartmouth, however, it looked as if he was returning to his old form.

But then there was another string of un-Jordanlike performances. Michael had just 8 points against Iowa, 11 against St. John's, and 10 versus Boston University. Once again help came from the family, this time from his father, who had watched almost every game Michael had ever played.

"You're trying to force things," James Jordan said. "You've got enough talent, so if you just play like Michael Jordan, things will fall into place."

Michael thought about what his father had said. He looked back at his first two Carolina years and again at his teammates. His father was right. He realized that he was playing with a slightly different mindset as a junior.

"I was trying too hard to live up to other people's expectations," he said, once again exhibiting an unusual amount of candor. "I was putting pressure on myself to be as good as people said I was. And maybe I was reading too much about myself, paying too much attention to my stats."

Whatever the cause, a more relaxed Jordan out on the court was the cure. Before long, Michael was again playing at an All-American level both offensively and defensively. And one of his patented offensive explosions was still a sight to behold.

Against LSU he had just three baskets in the first half. But in the second half he suddenly took off. First he took a lob pass from freshman guard Kenny Smith and jammed it home. Seconds later he switched roles, passing to Smith, who canned a jumper. Then a lightning-quick baseline drive resulted in a three-point play. Seconds later he brought the crowd to its feet with a spectacular flying dunk. That explosive sequence turned the game around, and from there the Tar Heels rolled. They won it 90–79, with Michael scoring 29 points.

Because the LSU game was on national television, Michael got even more exposure. More and more people were beginning to realize that this thin junior was simply a marvelous basketball player.

"Michael was just unreal," said teammate forward Matt Doherty. "He just took over and put on a show for the entire nation."

By this time, Michael's second-half eruptions were well known. He seemed to have the ability to elevate his game to still another level when the chips were down. His crunch-time performances were as much a testimony to his mental toughness as to his physical ability. In a game against Maryland, also on national

TV, Michael scored 19 of his 25 points in the second half, including 13 in the final 10 minutes to blow open what had been a hard-fought contest.

Once Michael came out of his slump, the Tar Heels picked up steam. This was another very solid Carolina ballclub, one that took its third straight Atlantic Coast Conference championship. They won the ACC tournament to enter the NCAAs with a 27-2 record. Many felt that the Tar Heels would once again win the national title, especially with Michael's proclivity for saving the best for last.

In the opening-round game against Temple, it was all Tar Heels. Michael was his usual self, hitting 11 of 15 from the floor and 5 of 7 free throws for 27 points as the Tar Heels topped the Owls, 77–66. It was a good start on what seemed like a serious run at the Final Four. But in the second round Carolina would have a tough nut to crack—Bobby Knight's Indiana Hoosiers.

It was a strange game in many ways. The tough Indiana defense prevented the Tar Heels from running, and once the Hoosiers controlled the tempo of the game, they were in the driver's seat. Michael had a rare off night and scored just 13 points. When the smoke cleared, the Hoosiers had knocked Carolina out of the NCAA tournament on the strength of a 72–68 victory.

Though the season had ended on a disappointing note, it had been another very successful year for Michael and his teammates. The Tar Heels finished at 28-3 overall, and no one can do much better than that. As for Michael, he had snapped his early-season slump to finish with a 19.6 scoring average. He also had Carolina bests of 55.1 percent shooting from the field and 77.9 percent from the free throw line. He was an All-American once again and for the second time in two years was named College Basketball Player of the Year.

Michael simply had gotten better as the year went on. From the time Carolina began its ACC season on January 7, Michael averaged 22.3 points and 6 rebounds over the next 18 games. In the final 10 games of the season his average was 24.1. Some people felt that in another style of offense, Michael could have averaged even more.

"I think Dean Smith's system helped Michael," said Fred Lynch, his junior high coach who has followed his career very closely. "It teaches discipline and also tells a ballplayer if he doesn't play defense, he's not going to play. From that standpoint, it made Michael into a much more well-rounded ballplayer.

"As a scorer who likes to freelance, the Carolina system probably held him back. If he had gone to North Carolina State, for instance, he probably could have easily averaged 28–30 points a game. But I really don't know if he would have been a better ballplayer if he went into a program like that."

Michael's scoring average at Carolina through his first three years was 17.7 points per game. While other great players have scored more than that during their college days, Bill Guthridge points out that Michael was always more interested in the team than in individual honors.

"Sure, Michael was capable of going out and scoring more points, but then we wouldn't have won as many games," Coach Guthridge said. "In college ball, the leading scorers in the country rarely come from the best teams in the country. We won as a team here,

Another award for Jordan. This one is the Eastman Award trophy, given to the nation's top collegiate player as voted by the National Basketball Coaches Association. Michael received this one in March 1984 after his junior year. *(AP/Wide World Photo)*

and Michael liked that. He wanted to win more than he wanted individual accolades. He worked to make himself a great defensive player and was named Player of the Year twice. So in that respect, I don't think our system held him back."

Michael certainly never complained. He enjoyed every minute of the show.

"Making the crowd and my teammates happy makes me happy," he said. "I love the game, I really do. I enjoy it, and I enjoy others enjoying it. I never think of it as a job."

But what of basketball as a job? For the first time since he had come to North Carolina, there was serious speculation about Michael leaving, declaring himself eligible for the NBA draft, and foregoing his senior year. James Worthy had done that very thing only two years earlier, and while Worthy had been only the second Carolina player to come out early (Bob McAdoo was the first), he had been very successful, immediately becoming an integral part of a powerful Los Angeles Lakers team.

For Michael Jordan, however, the decision wasn't an easy one. One of his goals had always been to graduate from college. He had remained a good student, maintaining a B average and continuing with geography as a major. Leaving that behind wouldn't be easy. Many college athletes who turn pro early say they'll return to complete their degrees; however, only a small percentage ever do it.

With Michael's great talent it seemed that he would only get better if he stayed another year. The only risk was the possibility of a debilitating injury. He had also voiced his desire to try out for the United States Olympic team that summer. In fact, George Raveling, who was slated to be an assistant coach for the Olympic team, was one of Michael's biggest boosters. Raveling felt Jordan could do almost anything.

"Michael Jordan is probably the best athlete playing college basketball," Raveling said. "He could be a great defensive back, a great center fielder, a great quarter-miler. And he has the potential to be a truly great basketball player, in a class with the Robertsons and Wests."

Oscar Robertson and Jerry West were still considered the Cadillacs of NBA guards, all-time great players who could do it all. It wasn't the first time Michael's name had been mentioned in the same breath as those two Hall of Famers. So the consensus was that Michael was ready. If he wanted to step into the pros, he could.

"I felt all along that Michael would be a better pro player than a college player," said Fred Lynch. "The reason is the nature of the game. There's no zone defense in the pros, and the more wide-open game will simply cater to his style."

But when Michael received the additional honor of being named *Sporting News* Player of the Year in March, he still hadn't declared himself eligible for the NBA draft, and the speculation was that he would be returning to Carolina, that he wouldn't come out. What the average fan didn't know, however, was that Dean Smith was a realist and would never try to hold a player back if he felt that player was ready for the NBA.

"Coach Smith always makes an interesting analogy when someone asks about a player coming out early," explained Bill Guthridge. "He says that if a student had just finished his junior year of business school and a company like IBM came in and offered him a million dollars to come to work for them immediately, that student could finish his degree in summer school. He would be foolish to say no, because it would be the best thing for him.

"It's the same with his athletes. His feeling is, the player should do what's best for him. During the season it's what's best for the team, but after the season it's what's best for the player. It was Coach Smith who recommended [that] Worthy come out early, and back in 1972 he recommended Bob McAdoo go. He also wanted Phil Ford to come out in 1977, but Phil wanted to stay in school and talked Coach Smith into staying. The coach also felt it was best for Sam Perkins to stay through his senior year, which Sam did."

Then what about Michael?

"Michael didn't really want to come out," Guthridge continued. "But Coach Smith thought he should. He felt Michael was ready for the pros, that it was best, because Michael could make a lot of money and get started on his pro career. We hated to lose him. In fact, we used to kid about it. While Coach Smith was advising him to go to the pros, we assistants were saying, 'Let's keep him, let's keep him.'"

Finally, on May 5, a news conference was held at Chapel Hill with Michael Jordan, as usual, the star. All the writers and reporters who gathered there knew what the announcement would be. College Basketball's Player of the Year was about to give up his final year of eligibility at North Carolina and make himself eligible for the NBA draft. Michael explained his decision.

"I don't owe the fans or alumni a last year at this university," said Michael, knowing that so many people wanted him to stay. "I have to do what's best for me. If I owe anyone, it's my parents, who have put up with me for 20 years.

"Money plays a big part in each one of our lives," he continued. "Who knows? I may not be around next year. I think it's better to start now. But this wasn't solely a financial decision. Here was a chance to move up to a higher level, make a better life for myself, and make me wiser about the life that is going on around me."

It obviously wasn't an easy decision. Michael had to weigh many factors, including his own desires and the wishes of his fans and family. Perhaps the deciding factor was getting the blessing of his coach, Dean Smith. So that was it. Instead of returning to North Carolina for the 1984–85 season, Michael Jordan would be taking his aerial act to the hallowed hardwoods of the National Basketball Association.

PART

THREE

CHAPTER 6

Rookie of the Year

Once Michael declared himself eligible for the draft, the speculation began. Would he be the league's top choice? Would he go in the top three? It was hard seeing him lasting beyond that. The consensus was that he was a can't-miss prospect, a player who hadn't yet reached the limits of his potential. In other words, many experts agreed with Fred Lynch—Michael Jordan would be an even better pro player.

But while the hoopla and excitement of Michael's decision was still settling, the youngster from North Carolina was preparing to live out another of his longtime dreams. He had been named to the United States Olympic basketball squad and was preparing for the summer games, which would be held that August in Los Angeles.

The coach of the U.S. squad was taskmaster Bobby

Knight of Indiana, a guy who expected players to listen and do things his way. He was vocal and sometimes abusive. But Knight was also a wily basketball man, and he knew that in Michael Jordan he had the crown jewel of Olympic basketball. He worked Michael into his system, but he also knew that when Michael took over a game, he wouldn't stop him.

Playing in front of pro-USA fans in Los Angeles, Michael didn't let them down. He popped in 14 points against China, scored 20 against Canada, and had 16 more in a win over Uruguay. Not only was he scoring, but he was doing it in such spectacular ways that Canadian guard Eli Pasquale just threw up his hands in frustration after losing to the USA team and said, "We just couldn't stay with Jordan."

No one could. Michael was on fire early against Spain, scoring 24 points in a 101–68 victory. Finally it came down to the gold medal game against a very good Brazilian squad. Before the final contest, Coach Knight talked to his team, then went up to the blackboard to chalk-in the starting lineup. There was a note taped to the board written by Michael Jordan. It read, simply, "Coach, after everything we've been through, there is no way we're going to lose this game."

If there was a chance of that happening, Michael Jordan simply wouldn't allow it. The Brazilian team was skilled and well coached, and in the first half they made it a ballgame. They also held Michael to just 2 points. But what they may not have known was that the second half almost always belonged to Jordan. Michael came on to score 14 second-half points, as the United States won the gold medal with an 87–79 victory.

The 1984 Olympics in Los Angeles saw Michael and his United States teammates win a gold medal. Other teams, such as the one from China pictured here, must have wondered why his tongue kept coming out of his mouth and whether that was the secret to the ball always going in the hoop. *(AP/Wide World Photo)*

Michael, as expected, was the USA's leading scorer —averaging 17.1 points a game—and had been the star of the team in more ways than one. And by the time the Olympics ended, something else had happened—the NBA draft had already taken place and Michael Jordan's professional fate was sealed.

The Houston Rockets had the first pick in the 1984 draft. They didn't surprise many people when they chose Akeem (now Hakeem) Olajuwon, a seven-foot center out of the University of Houston. Olajuwon, who was born in Lagos, Nigeria, was already an outstanding player and one that most experts felt would become a dominating NBA center, which he has. So it was no surprise that the Rockets took him, especially since he had also played his college ball in Houston.

But the second pick was a surprise. It belonged to the Portland Trail Blazers, a team that needed Michael's talents and charisma very badly. However, the Blazers surprised everyone by tabbing 7'1" center Sam Bowie of Kentucky. In his sophomore year of 1980–81, Bowie was considered a coming superstar. But he had missed two full years to leg injuries before returning to the Wildcats in 1983–84. Many considered him a medical risk (a prognostication that, unfortunately, turned out to be true) and a draft risk. When the Blazers took him, however, the team that was waiting to choose next breathed a long sigh of relief, before jumping for joy. The Chicago Bulls would now be able to get their man.

The announcement was simple: THE CHICAGO BULLS PICK MICHAEL JORDAN, GUARD, FROM NORTH CAROLINA. But the implications would be far-reaching.

Located in the Windy City, the Bulls were certainly a major-market franchise, but one that had had limited success since coming into the NBA as an expansion team in 1966. In a sense the franchise was a long time coming. In the early days of the NBA the town had the Stags, a team that lasted only from 1946 to 1950. Then in 1961 the Chicago Packers joined the league. They competed for a year, then disbanded. A year later there were the Chicago Zephyrs. That club also remained in the Windy City for just a season before moving to Baltimore and becoming known as the Bullets.

Chicago was then without a pro team until the Bulls were born in 1966. The franchise was far from a laughingstock. From 1970 to 1975 the team finished second in its division four straight times, then won a divisional crown. In 1971–72, the Bulls had a best-ever record of 57-25. That was a solid club, with the likes of Jerry Sloan, Chet Walker, Norm Van Lier, Tom Boerwinkle, and Bob Love. Good, but not great, the club always fell short at playoff time.

The team was up and down in the late 1970s and early 1980s. In the two years before Michael was drafted, the Bulls finished with records of 28-54 and 27-55, well out of the running for a playoff spot. In fact, the team hadn't been in the playoffs since 1981. These simply were not good teams. The Bulls seemed saddled with players who never lived up to their potential, were struck down by injuries, or beset by personal problems. There was no stability, no real star to build around, or leader to take charge.

Even the coaching situation was unstable, with four different head coaches in three years. To say that both the Bulls and the city of Chicago needed a Michael

Jordan was a gross understatement. The team welcomed him with open arms and an open wallet. He signed a seven-year, $6.15 million contract which, at that time, was reported to be the best pact ever given a guard in league history.

The contract guaranteed him $3.75 million for the first five years, starting at $550,000 for his rookie year and ending at $1 million in the fifth year. That was guaranteed. Then there were two nonguaranteed years at $1.1 million and $1.3 million, with the Bulls having the option. It wouldn't take long for the team to realize it had gotten a bargain.

Michael's representative, ProServ, Inc., felt its newest client would be even more valuable endorsing products. David Falk of ProServ explained it:

"In the age of TV sports, if you were to create a media athlete and star for the nineties—spectacular talent, midsize, well-spoken, attractive, accessible, old-time values, wholesome, clean, natural, not too goody two-shoes, with a little bit of deviltry in him— you'd invent Michael."

Before the year was out, Michael was in full swing endorsing products, beginning with a new basketball shoe from Nike called Air Jordan. But this wouldn't have been possible if Michael hadn't produced on the court, something he did from day one.

Former NBA guard Kevin Loughery was the Bulls' coach in 1984–85, and he quickly saw no need to put any restraints on his talented rookie. Unlike his college days, when he had to stay within Dean Smith's system, Michael was now able to freelance, to be more creative on the court, and to spend more time with the basketball in his possession. He scored almost at will, speeding past—and soaring over—veteran players

Michael would get used to having a battery of microphones in front of him and talking to a room full of reporters. But this occasion was special because it was the first, taking place in September 1984 after Michael signed his first professional contract. The Bulls gave him a seven-year deal and at the same time made him the third-highest-paid rookie in NBA history. *(AP/Wide World Photo)*

who began wondering if there was anything to stop this bolt of rookie lightning from North Carolina.

Michael's adjustment to NBA life seemed almost instantaneous. There have been just a handful of players who have excelled from day one, guys like Bill Russell, Oscar Robertson, Kareem Abdul-Jabbar, Magic Johnson, and Larry Bird. There are some others, too, but many players, including some of the great ones, have needed a period of adjustment.

When the Bulls took the court for their opening game against the Washington Bullets, Michael was in the starting lineup. He was joined by Steve Johnson and Orlando Woolridge at forwards, Caldwell Jones at center, and Ennis Whatley at the other guard. It was not a lineup that would challenge for the championship. The Bulls would win their opener, 109–93, with Woolridge scoring 28 points. Michael had a modest 16, but certainly gave flashes of things to come.

It didn't take long for those things to happen. In the team's third game, against the Milwaukee Bucks, the rookie from Carolina broke loose for 37 big points as the Bulls won again. Then a little over two weeks later, in the club's ninth game, he rattled the iron for 45 points in a winning effort against San Antonio.

But it wasn't just the amounts he was scoring, it was also the way he was doing it. Michael was all over the court—driving the middle, going baseline, hitting jumpers, rattling the rim with electrifying slam-dunks, putting on the kind of show that North Carolina fans saw only in occasional bursts or flashes. Now the extraordinary was becoming the norm. This was a rookie who was quickly rising to superstar status before the ink on his contract was dry.

"I never practice the fancy stuff," Michael told one

reporter. "If I thought about a move, I'd probably make a turnover. I just look at a situation in the air, adjust, create, and let instinct take over."

Part of the reason he was able to do all this was his tremendous hang time. While Michael was still soaring through the air it seemed that the other players were going up and coming down. And he always did it with his mouth open and tongue out—the old habit he had never shaken.

By the time the season reached the halfway mark, Michael was an All-Star, named as an alternate to the Eastern Division All-Star squad. He was also vying for the league lead in scoring with the Knicks' Bernard King and, incredibly, also leading the Bulls in rebounding, assists, steals, and minutes played. To find another NBA guard who entered the league with such all-around talent you'd have to go all the way back to Oscar Robertson in 1960. And what's more, the Bulls were playing almost .500 ball at 20-21.

The excitement over Michael Jordan continued to build. The Bulls' home attendance was up more than 80 percent from the year before. A Chicago television station that carried the Bulls' games reported that there were an additional 30,000 television sets tuned in to the games since Michael arrived. Even on the road, the team was drawing an average of over 4,000 fans per game more than it had the year before.

"Michael Jordan is already in a class by himself," said Phoenix Suns' marketing director Harvey Shank. "It's the way he gives himself to the game and his God-given talents. Michael Jordan coming to town is like a major entertainer appearing in Phoenix. People line up outside his locker room before warmups just to get a glimpse of him. I've been here since 1971, and one thing I've always admired is the way Julius Erving always related to the fans from the moment he arrived at the arena. Michael is the same kind of individual."

Posters were beginning to appear with Michael soaring through the air, tongue out. The player he was being most compared with was former All-Star Julius Erving, the great "Doctor J," who electrified fans in his early ABA years in the early 1970s and then later with the 76ers of the NBA. The Doc was just winding down his career when Michael came in and no longer flew through the air with the greatest of ease. But this new kid did, and the consensus was that Michael had a more total, all-around game than the Doctor.

Yet with all the instant fame and attention accorded him, Michael remained the same friendly, accessible performer he had always been, and not a guy resented by his teammates for hogging the spotlight.

"It would have been easy for people to resent him with all the points he scores, the publicity he gets, and the money he makes," said Bulls' center Dave Corzine. "But nobody does. Everything is there for him to be a jerk if he was that way, but he isn't. He just doesn't have that kind of personality. He works as hard in practice as he does in the games and hates to lose. And I've never heard him complain about anything."

Sound familiar, the guy who works hard in practice and hates to lose? Those were the same qualities Michael had since high school, and he remained unspoiled by fame and riches.

Another new teammate, veteran Orlando Woolridge, said that Michael's enthusiasm for the game and his work ethic were catching.

"He has an amazing flow of adrenaline," said Woolridge. "When he runs and leaps in practice we all want to try to run and leap with him, even if we are tired. It's been bump-and-grind time here for quite a while, and now the excitement level within the team is incredible. I'm so enthusiastic about him that my wife gets tired of hearing me talk about him."

Those were the kinds of comments Michael wanted to hear. He realized quickly that he was the focus, the guy people came to see, the new kid on the block, the newest star in the league. Yet he made up his mind to act a certain way during his rookie year and has carried that same posture right up to today.

"I've seen stars isolate themselves," Michael said. "Not me. I like to go to meals with the guys and pick up the tab. Like a quarterback with his linemen."

There was only one hint of controversy during Michael's rookie year, and it came at the NBA All-Star Game. Michael was already under contract to Nike. The Air Jordan basketball shoe would hit the stores in March, though Michael had been promoting them since the preseason. He also had a line of Nike sportswear in his name.

When he appeared at the slam-dunk contest the day before the All-Star Game, Michael was wearing gold chains and a Nike warmup suit. The rest of the NBA vets had their team warmup gear, and they felt that Michael was singling himself out by wearing his own line of clothing. Word got out that Michael was getting cocky and becoming a showboat.

"That was the most hurting thing in my whole career," said Michael, remembering the incident. "I didn't see any reason to be cocky, because there was nothing to be cocky about. My lawyers asked me to wear the Nike warmups during the dunk contest. I thought it was normal procedure. It was my first All-Star Game, and I didn't really know what was going on. Looking back now, I wouldn't have done it if I had known it would cause so much trouble."

It didn't end there. In the game itself, a number of players on both teams seemed determined to teach the rookie a lesson. His opponents played a rough brand of defense, and his teammates seemed reluctant to give him the ball. As a result Michael took just nine shots, while 43,000-plus fans at the Indiana Hoosierdome screamed for more. There was little doubt that Michael had been frozen out.

But was it really because of the warmup suit or because Michael, whose slam-dunk talents were considerable, was showing off? Maybe neither of those theories was the reason. Some speculated that a few NBA stars were jealous, that they resented the amount of publicity that a rookie was receiving. In just half a season Michael was perhaps the most sought-after player in the league and certainly its biggest drawing card. It's also a pretty safe bet that most of those vets didn't really know Michael Jordan, because as they began to know him in ensuing years, any resentment all but disappeared.

One of the players allegedly involved in the plot to teach Michael a lesson at the All-Star Game was a member of the Detroit Pistons. The next time the teams met, the player supposedly apologized to Michael. But Michael wasn't convinced the apology was sincere. That night he played like a man possessed, scoring 49 big points in a 139–126 Chicago overtime win. It was Michael's kind of payback, right out on the court. He didn't mouth off or complain about what had happened at the All-Star Game. He simply let his game speak for him.

Michael's 49-point night marked the 17th straight game he had led his team in scoring. Included in that run were games of 42, 36, 35, 38, 45, 38, 41, and 49 points. He was a player who was very difficult to stop. Another understatement. He was close to incredible.

The Lakers' Michael Cooper was a quick 6'6" swing man considered among the best defensive players in the league. Cooper was so good that he was often asked to cover the likes of Larry Bird, who stood three inches taller at 6'9". But when he covered Michael, or tried to cover him, it was different.

"When people say I do a good job on Michael, or that so-and-so did the job, that's wrong," Cooper said. "There's no way I can stop him. I need the whole team. As soon as he touches the ball, he electrifies the intensity inside you. The alarm goes off because you don't know what he's going to do. He goes right, left, over you, around and under you. He twists, he turns. And you *know* he's going to get the shot off. You just don't know when and how. That's the most devastating thing psychologically to a defender."

It would be difficult to find another All-Star-caliber defender talking about a rookie that way, but Cooper's description might have very well caught the essence of a defensive player's feelings when he had to face Michael Jordan.

Besides the individual heroics, Michael had accomplished something else in 1984–85. His presence had made a very mediocre Bulls team competitive. With

Explosive moves to the hoop are a Jordan trademark. Here he soars past the Lakers' Michael Cooper for the dunk, even though Cooper was considered one of the very best defenders in the NBA. *(AP/Wide World Photo)*

three games remaining in the season, Chicago had a record of 38-41. If they won all three, they would finish at .500. But by then even Michael couldn't work any more miracles. The team lost the final trio of games to finish at 38-44. That was still a major improvement over the previous season. The team's third-place finish in their division earned them a playoff berth for the first time since 1981.

Michael had produced a brilliant rookie season. He scored a team-record 2,313 points—most in the league, and good for a 28.2 average. He didn't win the scoring title, since the Knicks' Bernard King was averaging 32.9 points a game before going down with a knee injury after 55 games. Because the NBA scoring title is based on average, King was the top gun even though Michael had the most points.

But scoring wasn't all he did. He also led the ballclub in rebounding—grabbing 534 for an average of 6.5 per game—in assists, with 481, and steals, with 196. In the playoffs the Bulls were beaten by the Milwaukee Bucks in four games, even with Michael averaging 29.3 per contest. But all in all it had been a successful season, thanks to the super rookie from North Carolina.

It was really no surprise when the postseason honors began rolling in. For openers, Michael was named first team All-Eastern Division. He also won the Schick Pivotal Player of the Year award and the Seagram's NBA Player of the Year prize. In addition, the *Sporting News* named him Rookie of the Year and the NBA capped it off by also naming him its Rookie of the Year.

Could it have been any other way?

CHAPTER 7

Air Jordan Is Grounded

Things couldn't have looked better for Michael as his first professional season ended. Not only did he have tremendous success on the court, but his enormous popularity was making his off-court endeavors eminently successful as well. His basic agreement with Nike for the Air Jordan basketball shoe earned him the nifty sum of $2.5 million up front as well as a percentage of shoes sold.

By the time the shoes came on the market in March of 1985, Michael was basketball's hottest commodity. Nike sold more than $110 million worth of Air Jordans, some 2.3 million pairs at about $65 each, and also generated an additional $18 million in sales of Air Jordan athletic wear and flight bags. As one of Michael's representatives at ProServ said:

"Michael turned the entire shoe industry upside

down by himself. He outsold entire companies across the board."

The runaway success of the shoe and apparel line would bring Michael other long-term endorsement contracts from companies such as Coca-Cola, Wilson basketballs, McDonald's, Excelcior International (Time Jordan watches), and eventually Wheaties.

But none of that kept Michael off the basketball court for long. He continued to practice, working hard to improve his defense and hone his game for what he hoped would be an even better second season. The Bulls had made some changes in the front office. Jerry Krause took over as vice-president of basketball operations and also served as general manager. Stan Albeck was the new coach. With the exception of power forward Charles Oakley, the team was essentially the same. Yet the presence of Jordan in the lineup made them dangerous every game.

That notion was quickly reinforced, as the team won its first two games of the season. Orlando Woolridge broke loose for 35 points in the opener against Cleveland, and Michael scored 33 to kcy a victory over Detroit in game two. Then came the third game, an October 29 road contest against the Golden State Warriors. The Bulls would win that one too, giving the team a 3-0 start. Only, the price they paid for that victory would put a damper on the entire season.

For the first time in his career, Michael Jordan suffered a serious injury. It happened when he went up for one of his patented slam-dunks. Instead of coming down with his usual toe-to-heel landing, he hit the floor flat-footed. Immediately he knew something bad had happened. The official diagnosis was a break of the tarsal navicular bone in the left foot. Unofficially it could have meant an end to the Bulls' season. The doctors said that Michael would be out of action at least six weeks. For the Bulls that might have been an eternity. Without Michael, the team promptly lost eight of its next nine games.

But it wasn't only the team that suffered. The fans had been dying to see how Michael would improve on his high-flying act from his rookie year. And then there was the man himself. Michael Jordan suddenly found himself without his art, without the means to create, without the frenetic activity of basketball. In other words this was the first time someone had ever said to Michael, "You can't play!"

It wasn't easy for him, as he readily admitted to anyone who would listen. "I've never gone through anything like this before," he said. "And I don't really know how to deal with it."

The first thing he had to do was get used to the cast on his broken foot. Then he had to decide what to do while the foot healed. Some injured athletes stay with their teams, but Michael decided against it. He felt he would attract too much attention to himself and maybe distract his struggling teammates. The last thing they needed was an injured Jordan getting all the attention.

"They need their own identity" was the way he put it. "If I were with them, I'd take a lot of that away."

He was probably right. Without Michael in the lineup, the team continued to struggle. Players like Woolridge, Quintin Dailey, Oakley, Gene Banks, Sidney Green, Dave Corzine, and veteran George Gervin worked hard and put together some high-scoring games. But the team was weak defensively and didn't have anyone to take charge at crunch time. They continued to work hard, however, because they felt they still had a chance to make the playoffs. That was their major incentive.

As for Michael, he spent some time at his new home in Northbrook, Illinois, and a great deal of time back at Chapel Hill, where he visited friends and continued to study for his degree in geography. Michael wasn't one to waste time.

"I learned from this entire experience that you've got to be mentally tough," he said. "In the beginning, the days were going so slow that I found myself just sitting around, counting the minutes. I realized that I had to put my mind to work, keep myself occupied."

The original schedule called for the cast to come off about mid-December, with the hope that Michael could return to the lineup around Christmas. That would be the best present the Bulls and their fans could hope to have. Michael too. But then there was a setback. When the foot was examined in mid-December, Bulls' team physician Dr. John Hefferon saw that the bone had not healed sufficiently. It was decided that the cast would remain in place another two weeks.

By month's end the permanent cast was replaced by a lightweight "walking" cast. Now the Chicago papers were saying Michael wouldn't be back until February 1. Though the news wasn't good, Michael tried to remain optimistic.

"My foot felt a lot lighter when the cast came off," he said. "But my calf is so small, it looks like malnutrition on my left leg. It's going to take a while for me to get to the form I want. The left leg is my power leg. That's the one I leap off. I'm still not going to push myself, but I'm hoping to be back for the Lakers game."

The game to which Michael referred was scheduled for January 20. But then a late-January X ray showed that there were still some signs of the fracture. The healing process was painfully slow, and knowing how valuable a commodity Michael was, Bulls' management said that he wouldn't get clearance to play until the bone was fully healed.

A disappointed Michael left Chicago for Chapel Hill, and when he got there, he found he couldn't control himself any longer. He had to play basketball. He began working out against doctors' orders. By February he felt that the foot had healed enough for him to begin going harder, even though the Bulls didn't know what he was doing.

"I started gradually," he said of his clandestine workouts. "First I just took free throws, then began moving around and taking shots. Finally we got up a couple of two-on-two games, slow motion, then three-on-three. One day some of the guys began playing five-on-five, full court, and I just got involved.

"The toughest part was mental. I found myself asking, 'Should I be doing this?' But as I ran the court I couldn't feel anything wrong. And as I continued playing, I could tell part of my game was coming back. When I finally dunked, it felt just wonderful."

Coming down from that first rim-rattler, Michael made sure he landed on his toes. The foot felt fine, convincing him even more that the injury had been a freak accident, not an inherent weakness in the foot. But as Michael continued to pick up the pace of his Chapel Hill workouts, the word of what he was doing

Michael was the most explosive rookie to come into the NBA in years. One trip around the league and the crowds flocked to see his acrobatic scoring bursts. Even on the bench while taking a rare breather, the intensity in Michael continued to burn. Just look at it in his eyes. *(AP/Wide World Photo)*

filtered back to Chicago. When he heard the news, general manager Jerry Krause was livid. Michael's doctors and his attorney agreed with Krause that Michael just shouldn't be going it alone, without medical supervision.

"The doctors say there is a 5- to 10-percent chance of reinjury," Michael's attorney said. "Any chance, even a slim one, seems an unacceptable risk."

Michael still felt he was right. "If you had an investment that was 90 percent sure, wouldn't you take it?" he asked.

Investment may have been the proper word. Without Michael in the lineup, Chicago's attendance was down 10 to 15 percent. Plus, other teams were losing money when they played the Bulls without their star.

"A team like the Clippers might double their nightly average with Michael playing," said David Rosengard, the Bulls' director of marketing. "He's good for maybe another 8,000 fans in that arena. You just can't realistically replace something like that."

Funny how so much of today's sports focuses on the financial. Sure, Michael was a draw, the NBA's best since Magic Johnson and Larry Bird came into the league and put the Lakers and Celtics on center stage. But as an individual, Michael was Mr. Excitement. No one wanted to see him out of action for a long period, but at the same time no one wanted to take a chance on possibly curtailing his career. Yet Michael continued to be adamant. His feelings about the injury and his return weren't based on any financial picture. No, with Michael it was purely his love of the game and desire to return to the challenge of the competition.

"It was much better for me to work out at Chapel

Hill than in Chicago, where everyone would be watching me," he explained. "The people here have been helping me for a long time, and I didn't feel the kind of pressure I would have felt in Chicago. Now people are saying I'd be a fool for coming back this year. They feel I should wait until next season. But those people haven't experienced the game of basketball like I have. I love it like a wife or a girl. I certainly wouldn't do anything to jeopardize my career, but I feel I can play."

In a sense, it became a battle of wills. Bulls' owner Jerry Reinsdorf consulted with a number of doctors who examined Michael and said he should wait, probably until the 1986–87 season began in September. That would reduce the chance of reinjury to just 1 or 2 percent.

"There is a greater chance of reinjury if Michael comes back now," Reinsdorf said, "and the club feels he shouldn't take that chance. We are trying to get Michael to understand that the risk-reward ratio is way out of whack."

The debate continued. "For them it's a business decision," Michael said. "For me, the choice is mental. If I had to sit out the rest of the year, I would go crazy. I feel I want to test the foot now. Suppose I wait until September and reinjure it then. If that happens, I lose two years and I couldn't take that. I say let's try it now and see what's going to happen. If I reinjure it now, I'd be better able to deal with it."

Maybe the Bulls could refuse to activate Michael, but they couldn't stop him from playing in pickup games at Chapel Hill or anywhere else. He could certainly get hurt just as easily that way as in front of sellout crowds in the NBA. Finally the team gave in.

"The club has decided this is a personal decision, and we're not going to stand in his way," Reinsdorf said. "Michael was not following doctor's orders when he was in North Carolina. It's almost like he was forcing our hand. So if he's going to play, I think we're better off letting him play here so at least we can watch over him."

Michael repeated his claim that only he knew how the foot felt and it felt fine. "If I feel any pain at all, I'll abort the mission," he said.

There had been players in the league who had continual foot problems. The classic case was former All-Star Bill Walton who, after leading the Portland Trail Blazers to an NBA title in 1977, was plagued by repeated injuries to his left foot for nearly nine years.

Yet many admired Michael for his stand. With the escalating salaries being paid to top athletes, his earning potential was enormous. Here he was, however, willing to risk millions just to play in a handful of games at the tail end of a losing season. His first game back would be on the night of March 15 against the Milwaukee Bucks. Michael had missed 64 games. In his absence the Bulls were just 21-43. There was little doubt that his teammates would be glad to see him out on the court.

The only question was, would the foot hold up?

CHAPTER 8

Flying High

With 15,208 fans on hand at Chicago Stadium, Michael took his warmups with his teammates for the first time in four and a half months. He wasn't in the starting lineup and didn't get into the game until there was 5:59 remaining in the first half. All eyes were on him the first couple of times he touched the ball. And when he made his first move to the hoop, the place erupted.

Michael drove straight at 7'3" Bucks' center Randy Breuer, leaped high in the air, and stuffed the ball through the hoop despite Breuer's efforts to stop him. He landed on his toes and sprinted back downcourt with nary a limp. He would play just 14 minutes and score 12 points in a losing effort. But the bottom line was that he was back.

At first the Bulls watched his minutes carefully. His

foot was examined by doctors after three games, and there was no sign of reinjury, swelling, or stiffness. Everything seemed fine, just as Michael said it was. But Michael's minutes continued to be monitored, and the team lost the first five games in which he played.

Michael certainly wasn't holding back. In fact, when he was in there, he played like a man possessed. It was as if he was trying to make up for the 64 games he missed. Against Atlanta he had seven steals, five of them coming in one quarter. He admitted that at times he was "too hyper" on the court, watching the clock, because he knew he would be pulled. It wasn't long before he began lobbying for more time. But owner Reinsdorf expressed the concern that many people around the team felt.

"In my heart, I want to turn him loose," the owner said. "But I'm scared to death every time I watch him play."

Slowly, however, the minutes increased and so did the production. The Bulls still had a chance to clinch the eighth and final playoff berth in the conference. In a March 29 game against the New York Knicks Michael scored 24 points in limited playing time. It was the first time he led the club in scoring since his return. He would continue to lead them during the remaining seven games of the year. But the fight for playing time wouldn't end.

"The doctors said my foot wasn't ready for a full game," he said, "but I practice the way I play. I mean, I bust my tail for 90 minutes or two hours in practice, and I still had to beg to play in games. I felt I was being misled."

Bulls' coach Stan Albeck was the one caught in the middle of the dilemma.

"You see Michael out there doing these amazing things and you're happy to see them," Albeck said. "But if something happened to him it would be an awful thing. Nobody wants to be associated with the ending of Michael Jordan's career."

By early April Michael was up to 36 minutes, and the Bulls were making a push for the playoffs. Everyone knew why the team was still in the hunt. It was the presence of Jordan. His own contribution plus his effect on his teammates was obvious.

"How many superstars want to come back like that," Albeck remarked. "Michael begged to come back, while there are a lot of other guys who beg to sit out with a hangnail."

The Bulls clinched the playoff spot in the second-to-last game of the year, topping Washington 105–103 before a packed house of 18,869 fans. Michael had 31 points in that one, his best total since his return. The club lost their final game to finish with a 30-52 mark for the year. It was generally acknowledged that their playoff chances weren't good, but at least they had made it into the postseason.

As for Michael, he had come on strong to average 26.5 points over his final 10 games. Unbelievably, he had played in only 18 total contests, averaging 22.7 points for the year. But the numbers during his sophomore season were unimportant. It was his health that mattered the most. Now the Bulls would have to take the worst record of all the 16 playoff teams up against the Boston Celtics. The Celtics, led by Larry Bird, were considered the better team by far.

The only thing the Bulls had going for them was Michael Jordan. His injured foot had passed every test and finally all restrictions were off. He would be turned loose.

Though Michael was determined to make up for lost time, he would have to deal with Celtic guard Dennis Johnson, one of the best defensive players in the league and a guy who had made the NBA all-defensive team for eight consecutive seasons. Johnson took pride in his defensive prowess and certainly wouldn't make things easy for Michael.

The first game was held on April 17 in ancient Boston Garden. As expected, the Celtics produced a solid team effort, led by superstar Bird. What the Bulls gave them in return was their version of Superman, disguised as number 23, Michael Jordan. Michael was out of this world as he made Dennis Johnson look like no more than a pickup-game player.

Michael was virtually unstoppable, going around and over Johnson repeatedly, then challenging the likes of Robert Parish, Kevin McHale, and Bird. He hit on a variety of drives, jumpers, and dunks, drawing *oohs* and *ahhs* from the partisan Boston crowd. He had 30 points in the first half alone, and when the game ended, he had impressed everyone with an incredible 49-point performance. Unfortunately, the Celtics still had their predicted victory, 134–104. But Michael had shown everyone he was all the way back.

"I want to win very badly," he said afterward. "My whole season is wrapped up in these playoffs. I want to do the things I couldn't do all season. When you're out of sight, people tend to forget you. I'm a competitor and I like to be respected as a player."

Not to worry. If anyone had the kind of short

memory that could forget Michael Jordan, he quickly let them know he was not only back, but back with a vengeance. And if they didn't get the message in game one, he taught it again in the second game—only better. Playing once more at Boston Garden, Michael took up where he left off, scoring almost at will and in often spectacular fashion.

The Bulls made sure to run a number of isolation plays in which the other four players moved to one side of the court, isolating Michael on a single defender with the room to go one-on-one. Michael was almost like a kid with a new toy. After that long layoff, it was as if he had just been introduced to the basketball and the fun of putting it through the hoop. When he hit two foul shots at the end of regulation to tie the score at 116–116, he had already scored 54 points.

Once again the Celtics prevailed, 135–131 in double overtime. But the talk of the basketball world was all Michael Jordan, who had riddled the tough Boston defense for an incredible 63 points. Michael played 53 minutes, hit 22 of 41 shots from the floor and 19 of 21 from the foul line. It was almost as if the Celtic victory was a given, because everyone wanted to talk about Jordan.

"As you can see, no one can guard him," remarked Dennis Johnson.

Larry Bird quipped that the Bulls player who scored 63 points was "God disguised as Michael Jordan."

Chicago coach Stan Albeck said, "This has to be the greatest individual performance in playoff history."

It almost didn't matter when the Celtics eliminated the Bulls in the third game, 122–104. Michael had "only" 19 in that one, but still averaged 43.7 points in the series. He had shown that he was completely recovered from the broken foot. But that wasn't all. Michael Jordan had used the three-game playoff series to give the basketball world a warning. He was again healthy and still hadn't completely tapped the vast potential of his talent. In other words, the best was yet to come.

The problem was that Michael's best versus that of the rest of the Bulls left a lot to be desired. The Bulls as a team still lacked stability. The other players didn't have the firepower to back their superstar. Besides Michael, the only player on the 1986–87 team who was close to being an All-Star was power forward Charles Oakley. But his forte was defense and rebounding. Otherwise, mediocrity was the order of the day. Get deeper into the bench, and the problems multiplied. In addition, the team had its third coach in three years as Doug Collins took over from Stan Albeck.

Under those conditions, stability was hard to find. Yet despite all the problems, Michael Jordan was about to put on a sterling performance for 82 games, perhaps the closest thing to a one-man show that the NBA had ever seen.

Michael had even agreed to take it somewhat easy over the summer to make sure that the foot remained sound. He began playing 18 holes of golf each day instead of intense pickup basketball games. In doing so, he found a new way to relax. It wasn't long before golf became a second love to him. Michael reported to training camp in tremendous physical condition. The results of the standard preseason medical tests showed that Michael's body contained only 3.29 percent body fat, an incredibly low amount, even for a trained athlete.

The Bulls' opening game was in New York, against the Knicks, and that was the night Michael Jordan served notice on the rest of the league that he meant business. With the huge Madison Square Garden crowd urging their team on, the Knicks took a 90–85 lead midway through the fourth period. They seemed to be gaining momentum, so the Bulls called time out. New coach Collins was busy outlining strategy, when Michael suddenly interrupted him.

"Coach," said Michael. "Don't worry. I'm not going to let you lose your first game."

Back on the court, Jordan went on one of his patented offensive explosions. He made the Knicks look as if they were standing still, driving around them, leaping over them, and popping jump shots from every angle. When the smoke cleared, Michael had scored 21 fourth-quarter points to bring the Bulls home with a 108–103 victory. For the entire game he had hit on 15 of 31 shots from the floor and 20 of 22 from the line, for 50 points. He was on his way.

As hard as it was to believe, Michael's physical attributes seemed better than ever. He looked quicker, stronger, and sharper, and he even seemed to be jumping better. He talked about a late-game dunk against the Knicks, saying, "I was close to eye level with the rim. Sometimes you just hit your wrists on the rim, but this time it was my elbows and everything. I almost overdunked the whole rim."

Whatever Michael was doing, it soon became obvious he wasn't about to stop. He followed his 50-point opener with a 41-point performance against Cleveland. Then, beginning in the eighth game of the year,

Back on the court following his injury, Michael took a back seat to no one. Here he drives around the Spurs' Gene Banks for 2 of his 45 points on the night. In typical fashion, he scored 16 of them in the final session to help the Bulls to a 120–117 victory. *(AP/Wide World Photo)*

when he popped for 48, Michael scored 40 or more points in 13 of the next 16 games, including a run of nine 40-plus games in a row. He was doing it all, and his heroics were keeping the Bulls right around the .500 mark. Needless to say, he had jumped to the top of the NBA scoring parade.

It seemed that in each and every game Michael did something special. There was a November 21 contest with the Knicks in Chicago. Air Jordan would pop for 40 points, but it was what he did in the final seven minutes that lit up the night. He wound up winning the game with a 20 footer from the corner with one second left, giving the Bulls a 101–99 victory. But that shot also represented his 18th straight point, a scoring streak that set an NBA record. It was almost like the game against New Hanover High in which he scored Laney's final 15 points. Now it was the NBA, and he was still doing it.

In April, against Atlanta, he would break his own record by scoring 23 straight points as part of a 61-point night. Sacramento Kings' assistant coach Jerry Reynolds put it this way:

"Every time you see him, he does something different. You might see other players and think they're just as good. Then you see Jordan again and say 'no way.' The other guys put on a great show, but Michael takes it to another level."

Air Jordan was the only reason the Bulls stayed around the .500 level and made the playoffs again. The team finished the season in fifth place, but with a 40-42 record. A look at Michael's numbers tells why.

He won his first scoring title with a 37.1 average, topping runner-up Dominique Wilkins by 8.1 points. His 82-game total of 3,041 points made him the only

NBA player besides Wilt Chamberlain to score more than 3,000 points in a season. He was also the first to have more than 200 (236) steals and over 100 (125) blocks in the same year. He led the Bulls in scoring in 77 of the team's 82 games and scored 40 or more points 16 times and 50 or more on 8 occasions.

Once again the Bulls had to take on the Celtics in the playoffs, and once again they were beaten in three straight. Not surprisingly, Michael had a great series even in defeat, averaging 35.7 points, 7 rebounds, 6 assists, and 2.3 blocks a game. It was his greatest season, but for the first time fans began wondering when Chicago management would complement their superstar with some other players who could really make the team a winner.

Michael couldn't do it alone, but he was sure flying high.

CHAPTER 9

Most Valuable Player

Help was on the way in 1987–88. The Bulls drafted a pair of promising forwards in 6'10" Horace Grant and 6'7" Scottie Pippen, two players with natural talent. How much they would contribute as rookies was hard to say. Veterans John Paxson, Rory Sparrow, and Sedale Threatt were on hand to help Michael in the backcourt. Charles Oakley was still a force at power forward, while Dave Corzine was competent, though not outstanding, at center. Help in the middle and bench strength seemed to be the team's major problems as they prepared for the new campaign.

Michael would be entering his fourth season, and there was little doubt remaining about his celebrity status. He was included among 70 new entries in the 1988 edition of the World Book Encyclopedia. According to encyclopedia editors, to become an entry "a person, event, or subject must have historical significance, must have made a major contribution to his or her field, or must be a topic of great interest to a large number of people."

In a sense, Michael was all of the above. In addition to stories about him in newspaper sports pages and all the sports magazines, feature stories about him appeared in such diverse publications as the *Wall Street Journal* and *Gentlemen's Quarterly,* which is essentially a fashion magazine.

His fans were interested in any tidbits about his personal life. For instance, they knew he had made good on his word and completed his degree in geography from North Carolina. He had come to love playing golf and even had a six-hole artificial putting green in the basement of his home. He was among the most courteous of athletes in dealing with the public and media, as well as one of the most accessible for a star of his magnitude.

But because he was so highly visible and well known, much of his private life was gone.

"Michael is almost a cult figure," said Jerry Krause. "He has no private life. I really feel for him. He gets mobbed all the time."

It was tough for Michael to go out in public, especially in Chicago, because of the crowds he attracted. Even Coach Collins called it "a lonely life. There is a time when you like to sometimes sit down in a movie with four or five of your buddies, eat some popcorn, laugh, and have a good time. That's taken away from you when you're as popular as Michael," said his coach.

Yet on the court he was still all competitor. Because

Coach Collins lost track of the score during a scrimmage, an angry Jordan stormed off the court.

"I'm a competitor and I want to win," Michael said of the incident. "I always keep score in everything—scrimmages, games, whatever—and I know the score was 4–4. Doug said it was 4–3, my team losing. . . . People may think this is all trivial, but when you're a competitor and want to win, nothing is trivial."

That was the key. Though Michael continued to exude an almost boyish joy in the challenge of the game or in a particularly difficult move or crowd-pleasing dunk, the bottom line was still winning. He had hated losing since his high school days and hated it even more as a pro. An NBA championship was his goal. He would ultimately settle for nothing less.

Michael Jordan would solidify his reputation as one of the great players in basketball during the 1987–88 season. When it ended, even more people referred to him as the best ever, a player who could do it all with a talent, style, and excitement that elevated the sport to a new level. By the time the year had ended, Michael's presence had elevated the Bulls to a level few people thought they could attain.

In fact, the Bulls had to be the surprise team of the NBA. With basically the same club that hit the court a year earlier, the Chicagoans exploded out of the gate. They won seven of their first eight and 12 of their first 15 games. Rookies Grant and Pippen had obvious talent, but Coach Collins was working them into the lineup slowly. What was the difference then? No one had to guess. A completely healthy and hungry Michael Jordan was tearing up the league.

He would tear it up all year, at both ends of the

court. Not only was Michael his usual, dynamic, often unbelievable self on offense, but he was also playing brilliant defense, not an easy thing to do. With the tremendous energy he used on his drives and dunks, and banging bodies with bigger guys under the hoop, it would have been understandable if he let up a bit at the other end. But in 1987–88, Michael's defensive play was better and more sustained than it had ever been.

The team hit a little skid in December, then picked up the pace again in January. Michael, of course, was again a starter at the midseason All-Star Game and won the league slam-dunk contest held the day before the game. He had promised his Bulls teammates he would split the $12,500 first prize with all of them if he won. Because he never acted superior to, or apart from, his teammates, they never resented all the attention he received, and they worked hard to support his incredible effort.

With Michael leading the way, the team won 18 of its final 25 games to finish with a surprising 50-32 record, good for second place in the Eastern Conference Central Division. It was the Bulls' best record since 1974–75. The entire team could be proud of its achievement, but what Michael Jordan had accomplished was even more amazing.

Michael won his second-straight scoring crown with 2,868 points in 82 games, an average of 35.0 points per contest. But while his average was down two points from the year before, his shooting percentage was up from 48.2 to 53.5. In addition, he had his usual number of spectacular games, going over 40 points 16 times and over 50 on 4 occasions, with a high of 59 against arch rival Detroit on April 3. He was also the Bulls' leading scorer in 81 of the team's 82 games.

And that wasn't all. Once the smoke cleared, Michael learned he had scored a unique double. He was named the NBA's Most Valuable Player as well as its Defensive Player of the Year, a combination never before achieved by a single player in the same season. In addition, he was a first-team All-Star, a starter on the all-defensive team, and the MVP of the All-Star Game. The pride he felt in his accomplishments was reflected in his comments on being the Most Valuable Player.

"It's a thrill, and I'm really happy," he said. "Winning this award has always been one of my biggest goals in basketball. It is a similar feeling to winning College Player of the Year. But this means a little more because of the caliber of the athletes. You're talking about 276 of the best athletes in the world. Now you are the MVP. That doesn't happen too many times."

His only disappointment was in the playoffs, although the Bulls showed improvement in postseason play. They took their first-round series by defeating the Cleveland Cavaliers, 3-2, before being eliminated by the tough Pistons, 4-1. Michael was a 36.3 scorer in 10 playoff games, keeping up his tradition of usually scoring at a higher clip in the playoffs than during the regular season. But the loss hurt.

Yet nothing could diminish the kind of season Air Jordan had put together. In addition to everything else, he also led the league in steals with 259, and his 131 blocked shots represented more blocks than 16 starting centers in the league had.

"People see me as just a scorer, somebody who

Michael and wife, Juanita, beam with pride after Air Jordan received his second NBA Most Valuable Player Award in 1991. The first came in 1987–88 when the five-time scoring champ averaged 35 points a game. *(AP/Wide World Photo)*

shoots a lot and doesn't do much else," Michael said after the season. "So this year I was determined to show my all-around game."

He had. His peers knew it, as did most astute observers of the game. Only the casual fan might have seen him as only a scorer. The others knew he was playing the game at an all-around level perhaps never seen before. A former teammate, Sidney Green, who was with the New York Knicks in 1987–88, felt that Michael had become a better ballplayer in another way.

"Michael is a much more mature ballplayer," said Green, "and that can be seen in his court awareness and his shot selection. He also respects the roles of his teammates."

That part was very important. Michael's talent was so great that his teammates often found it difficult to keep up with him. Despite his great individual moves and his ability to take over a game almost singlehandedly, Michael was very aware of his teammates, their limitations and abilities. He worked hard to get the most from their talents, and his teammates knew it.

In the playoffs Michael had scored 50 and 55 points against the Cleveland Cavaliers, prompting the Cavs' outstanding guard Ron Harper to marvel at his stamina.

"The thing is that Mike doesn't get tired," said Harper. "I know I get tired in the fourth quarter, but he doesn't. He justs gets stronger and keeps responding."

That, too, is a quality only the great ones have. In just four years, Michael Jordan had accomplished more than most do in a career. It didn't seem there was much he could do for an encore—except continue to pursue that elusive NBA championship.

The Bulls needed more quality players and the chemistry to allow those players to work with Michael without hampering his game. Not easy. But management was trying. In June the team made a bold move. They traded power forward Charles Oakley, one of the best rebounders in the league, to the New York Knicks for veteran center Bill Cartwright.

Cartwright was a 7'1", 245-pounder who had a solid season in 1987–88 after being hampered by foot problems the previous two years. But "Mr. Bill," as he was called, was nearly 31 and perhaps on the downside. It was a risky deal. As insurance, the team then made 7'0" Vanderbilt center Will Perdue its first pick in the college draft and shortly after the season began traded for veteran guard Craig Hodges, a good long-range shooter.

There was one other matter to be settled before the new season got underway. Because basketball salaries had been escalating rapidly, the long-term contract Michael had signed as a rookie had become anachronistic. What had seemed like a huge salary in 1984 was out of step with the monies being paid other star players now. And Michael was the star of stars.

"Clearly the market is changing," said David Falk, Michael's business representative. "We were very excited about the deal back in 1984, but it's a case of what seems high today doesn't seem high down the road."

Michael had earned $800,000 in 1987–88, but a few players, such as the Lakers' Magic Johnson and the Knicks' Patrick Ewing, were over the $2 million mark, and a number of others were between $1.5 and $2 million. Michael said that he would honor the terms of his original contract, but added:

"If you are a concerned owner and an owner that looks after the best interests of his players, then it's [a new contract] something you would do on your own without the player really threatening to [sit out], if you consider that individual to be among the elite class."

Michael had chosen his words carefully. Bulls' management got the message. Knowing full well Michael's value to the team and the franchise, he was given a new eight-year pact worth an estimated $25 million. It was also estimated that with deferred payments, Jordan's estimated annual salary would be in the $3.125 million range. No matter what the size of the contract, there was one thing the Bulls didn't have to worry about—Michael would be the same all-out performer night after night, week after week, that he had always been. He knew no other way to play.

The team had a different look as the 1988–89 season began, and it obviously took a period of adjustment for everyone. Whereas the 1987–88 club was 12-3 after 15 games, this Bulls team was just 7-8 despite Michael, who had already scored 52 points in each of three different games. Grant was still working in at power forward, while Pippen was recovering from back surgery and being slowly put back into the lineup.

Cartwright was a steadying influence at center, but wasn't the scorer he had been early in his career and was sometimes prone to foul trouble. Though he was a wily and tough defender, "Mr. Bill" also wasn't a great rebounder, and the club missed Oakley's board work. So once again it was Michael Jordan who had to carry the brunt of the load. He was in his usual spot as the league's leading scorer and again doing it on both ends. For the first time some began questioning whether he was doing too much, whether his body could take the pounding. Many of his twisting, turning drives resulted in his being knocked hard to the floor. And when he rebounded, he was going up against players outweighing him by 40 or 50 pounds.

"I don't really feel the pain all that much on a day-to-day basis," Michael said. "I feel it after games, which is normal. But there are times when I feel like I've been playing in this league eight years instead of five."

He did admit, however, that he was making one concession to the years and the pounding. "I haven't been going to the hoop as much as I did in the past," he said. "I've been shooting more from the outside to avoid some of the banging you get going to the basket."

In a January 25 game against Philadelphia, Michael reached another milestone—scoring his 10,000th career point, a number he reached faster than any player in history, with the exception of Wilt Chamberlain. But while the individual honors were great, he was still more concerned with getting the team back on track. During January and February the Bulls began coming on, raising their record from 15-12 to 33-21 over a two-month period. They still weren't among the NBA's elite, but they were getting closer.

The ballclub finished the year at 47-35 and in fifth place, but only three games behind the pace of the second-place team of a year earlier and in the playoffs once again. In addition, they were a much better team at the end of the season. Grant was an improving power forward and Scottie Pippen, recovered from surgery, looked to be a coming star at the small forward slot.

As for Michael, it had been another typical season for him. He was the scoring champ with a 32.5 average and had his best rebounding year ever, grabbing 652 caroms for an average of 8.0 a game. Not many guards this side of Magic Johnson can rebound like that. In addition, he was an All-NBA first-team choice and an All-Defense first teamer. That was almost an automatic now. Schick named him as their Pivotal Player of the Year and he was the *Sporting News* Player of the Year as well. The Lakers' Magic Johnson was the league's MVP, though many cast their vote for Michael.

The comparison with Magic is an interesting one. Many consider the Laker great a player who changed the game, showing everyone that a 6'9" athlete could play point guard. Magic's all-around skills, though considerable, probably fall somewhat short of Michael's. But Magic has led the Lakers to five world championships since coming into the league in 1979. Though the Lakers had a great overall lineup throughout the 1980s, Magic's role with the L.A. team is another mark of his greatness. He's been their leader, and that's what every competitive athlete wants the most.

Perhaps that's the reason Michael Jordan is always at his best in the playoffs. It was no different in 1988–89. Only, this time the Bulls began making their mark as a team. Chicago's first opponent was the Cleveland Cavaliers, a team that had a 57-25 record in the regular season and had beaten the Bulls in all six games the two teams played. No wonder the Cavs were heavy favorites.

One of the raps against the Bulls in the past was that the other players sometimes depended too much on Michael, figuring he would get the job done by himself. Even G.M. Jerry Krause remarked that Michael sometimes dominated to the extent that his team would develop a let-him-do-it attitude. But when the Bulls whipped the Cavs, 95–88, in the opener at Cleveland, there were signs that things were changing.

Cleveland won the second game, but in the third Michael had 44 points to key a 101–94 Bulls win. The Cavs took the fourth despite a 40-plus effort by Jordan, but in the fifth and deciding game in Cleveland, the Bulls really came of age. They scrapped and fought the whole way, keeping the ballgame close, not allowing the Cavs to take advantage of their home court. Finally it came down to this: Cleveland had a 100–99 lead with three seconds left, it was do or die for the Bulls, and everyone knew who would take the final shot.

The Bulls inbounded at midcourt and got it to Michael. He dribbled to his right, then switched hands and moved quickly to the left, going up with the jumper around the free throw line. The Cavs' Craig Ehlo had a good angle and went for the ball. But Michael double-pumped and with that great hang time shook loose from Ehlo and let the shot go. It hit the back of the rim and—dropped through. The Bulls had won the game—and the series—101–100.

In the next round Michael again did his thing, against the New York Knicks. He got solid help from his teammates and Michael and the Bulls won the best-of-seven series, 4-2. In Game 4, Michael had 47 points, and in the sixth and final game he canned a pair of free throws with four seconds left to give his team a 113–111 victory. His 40 points led the scoring parade. He was quickly becoming the marvel of the entire sports world.

"Michael's the best," said boxing champ Sugar Ray Leonard. "I live vicariously through him."

Suddenly the upstart Bulls were in the Eastern Conference Finals, a step away from the championship round. Their opponents were the rough-tough Detroit Pistons, led by guards Isiah Thomas and Joe Dumars, and the man considered by many the league's best defensive player, Dennis Rodman. The Pistons were on their way to the NBA title, and after losing two of the first three to Chicago, they pulled their act together to win the final three games, and the series.

The Pistons probably defense Michael as well as anyone, often muscling him with their rough style of play. Yet when the season ended, he had still averaged 34.8 points for 17 playoff games. So while the bad news was that the Bulls had lost, the good news was that they were getting closer. Maybe next year, everyone thought.

Despite the loss to the Pistons, the legend of Michael Jordan continued to grow. One Chicago sportswriter said, "Michael remains the athlete of the '50s amidst the athletes of the '80s," pointing out that he never complains, hasn't let his great fame change him, and answers reporters' questions politely and patiently. He also visits sick kids in hospitals and is involved in the Just Say No to Drugs program.

His mother, Delores, told a reporter how Michael had once stopped on his way home from a game to give the Air Jordan sneakers he was wearing to a street kid, but only after making the boy promise to go to school the next day.

"Michael is all about giving back" was the way Mrs. Jordan put it.

CHAPTER 10

The Quest to Be the Best

He was back on the court in 1989–90, trying to give back to the fans of Chicago and his teammates. His quest remained the same—that elusive NBA championship. There were a few more changes. The team drafted center-forward Stacy King from Oklahoma and guard B. J. Armstrong out of Iowa. And they also had a new coach, Phil Jackson, a former Knicks player who had served his apprenticeship as a head coach in the Continental League and then as an assistant with the Bulls the past two seasons.

In the opening game, a 124–119 overtime win against Cleveland, Michael scored 54 points. He seemed better than ever. A sellout crowd of 18,676 fans jammed Chicago Stadium. All 82 regular-season Bulls' games, home and road, would be sellouts, another tribute to an improving team and to the most exciting player of his time.

It was a banner season. The Bulls finished second to Detroit in the Central Division with a 55-27 record. Michael, of course, led the way with yet another absolutely brilliant season. But this time he had real help from a real team. These Bulls were no longer a one-man show, though the one man was still there whenever he was needed.

The team was becoming very solid. Horace Grant had his best year ever at power forward. Pippen became an all-star in his own right. He was the team's second-highest scorer and a guy who could do it at both ends. Despite his increasing age, Bill Cartwright was still a wily center and getting help from young Will Perdue. John Paxson was a solid starter, and the bench was continuing to pick up strength.

Michael was, of course, still the main man. He won his fourth-straight scoring title with a 33.6 average, led the league in steals for the second time, and had his usual first-team spot on the All-NBA team and all-defensive squad. His scoring bursts were now also legendary. Though NBA fans had been watching him do his thing for six years, they still marveled at his Air Jordan act. On numerous occasions Michael would drive to the hoop, get hammered by a defender, and as he was going down throw up a shot from an awkward, almost impossible, angle. And the ball would go in! Fans who watched him hundreds of times came back for more. And he gave it to them.

He had 21 games of 40 or more points in 1989-90 and on March 28, in an overtime win against Cleveland, he threw in a career-best 69 points. Led by Michael's superb play, the Bulls had a 27-8 record

after the All-Star break—second best in the league—
and also had a team-record 15-game home win streak
and eight-game road win streak.

But there was still the matter of the playoffs. This
time the Bulls had to be considered serious contend-
ers. When they made quick work of the Bucks in four
games it was expected. Next came the Philadelphia
76ers and their great star, Charles Barkley. But as
great as Barkley was, center stage belonged to Michael
Jordan.

The Bulls took the first two games in Chicago,
111–97 and 109–92, as Michael scored 39 and 45
points. Back in Philly, the Sixers prevailed in Game 3,
118–112, despite a 49-point effort by Michael, including 24 points in the fourth period. It was the fourth
game, however, that really pointed up how the Bulls
had matured as a team.

For nearly three periods it was all Philadelphia.
Late in the session, the Sixers had a solid 80–66 lead.
But then the Bulls began coming on. Early in the
fourth period the Philly lead was down to 89–80.
Chicago was getting outstanding play from reserves
Ed Nealy and B. J. Armstrong. And, of course,
Michael was there, as usual. He scored 18 fourth-
quarter points as the game ended in the Bulls' favor,
111–101.

Michael had another of those games that were
becoming the norm rather than the exception. He
wound up with 45 points, 11 assists, 6 rebounds,
2 steals, and 2 blocks, as well as shutting down
Philly's high-scoring guard, Hersey Hawkins, in the
final session.

"Nobody has ever been better at the end of game

than Michael," said Coach Jackson. "Oscar Robertson was great, but this guy is a closer at both ends."

Back in Chicago, the Bulls closed out the Sixers easily, 117–99. Now, for the second straight year, the team was in the Eastern Conference finals. And once again they would have to go up against the Detroit Pistons, the defending NBA champions. The Pistons were tough on Michael. While no team could completely stop him, the defense-minded Pistons did a better job than any other team in the league.

According to Pistons' coach Chuck Daly, the Detroit resolve to ground Air Jordan began on April 3, 1988, when Michael went wild to the tune of 59 points against the Pistons in a nationally televised game.

"We made up our minds right then and there that Michael was not going to beat us by himself again," said Daly. "We had to commit to a total team concept to get the job done."

The Pistons devised a defense in which each player on the court had part of the responsibility to stop Jordan. It was a defense different from any other, and the individual responsibilities became collectively known as the "Jordan Rules." The defense was in some ways technical, in other ways physical. In other words, when in doubt, knock him to the court. That, too, happened on more than one occasion.

Most of the responsibility fell to guard Joe Dumars and forward Dennis Rodman. Michael described Dumars as a "strong, physical, and sound player" who "doesn't do anything spectacular, but gets the job done." Rodman, he said, is "a kind of flopper [a player who is always falling down and trying to draw a charging call], and he gets some calls. But he's got very quick feet and he can get away with playing me that close. Sometimes."

Former Bulls' coach Doug Collins said that Dumars was the key.

"You must have that initial guy, a guy like Dumars, to accept the physical and mental challenge of playing Michael," Collins said. "If you don't, Michael will kill you, regardless of how great your principles are."

Fortunately for the Pistons, they not only had a plan, but the best defensive team in the league to carry it out. No one player or one team really stops Michael, but the Pistons managed to keep him in check just enough to win. Once again, the rest of the Bulls had failed to pick up the slack, something that didn't make Michael happy. Still, it took Detroit the full seven games to finally eliminate the Bulls. The Pistons then went on to win their second consecutive NBA championship.

But the Bulls gave them a real scare. After the Pistons won the first two in Detroit, it looked like a quick series, until some real prodding from Michael helped his team come alive.

"As a leader, I've never been critical or cursed any of my teammates," he said. "The rumors said I did, but I did not. I always spoke in terms of 'we.'" One reporter, however, said that an angry Jordan had snapped to him that "if my teammates think I'm going to carry them again, they're wrong!"

Exactly what he said may never be known, but the rest of the Bulls knew he wasn't happy with their play in the first two.

"He said the guys were playing lousy ball," admitted Horace Grant. "He didn't want to name names, but he was right. The guys know who they were. We were embarrassed. Mike feels the guys aren't giving their all, and I don't blame him. . . . We played terribly. I've never seen Michael that upset."

Coach Phil Jackson admitted he was sometimes surprised that Michael could keep his feelings to himself so often.

"Anyone who was offended by what he said can't have a conscience," said Jackson. "I don't think they could have been offended. Surprised, maybe. Michael usually keeps his feelings and frustrations to himself."

It was said that Michael was tired of hearing that the Bulls were a one-man team, yet that seemed the case over and over again. His tirade was intended to get the attention of his teammates.

"What Michael did was a wake-up call for us," Scottie Pippen said. And Coach Jackson added, "When the captain demands something out of his club, it is his prerogative. He has the right. If we can't take a little adversity, we are not in the hunt the right way."

Michael had scored 34 in the first game, but just eight in the second half. In the second game he had a sore left hip and right wrist and scored just 20. That was the game in which he got little backup, helping to set off his outburst. But Game 3, back in Chicago, was different. Michael exploded for 47 points, including 31 in the second half and 18 in the fourth quarter, as the Bulls won, 107–102. Scottie Pippen chipped in with 29 and reserve Ed Nealy played a key role off the bench. Horace Grant had 10 points and 11 rebounds, crediting Michael with the turnaround.

"I think Michael has given us confidence," he said.

But defending NBA champs are never easy to beat. The Bulls won the fourth game, 108–101, but back in

Early in the 1990–91 playoffs, Michael and the Bulls showed they were ready to go all the way. Here Michael makes it look easy as he speeds past the Knicks' Gerald Wilkins on the way to yet another slam dunk. The Bulls won this one, 89–79, behind Jordan's 26 points. *(AP/Wide World Photo)*

Detroit the Pistons prevailed again, 97–83. The Bulls kept it an all–home court series by taking Game 6 in Chicago easily, 109–91, setting up a seventh and deciding tilt. The Bulls were just a game away from going to the NBA finals for the first time.

Unfortunately, it turned out to be a Detroit night. Playing before a wild home crowd, Detroit was not to be denied. It didn't help that Scottie Pippen came down with a migraine headache that totally reduced his effectiveness. Pippen had averaged 19 points and 6.7 rebounds in the first six, but in the finale he had just two points and four boards. Guard John Paxson also had to sit out, with a bad ankle sprain. So while Michael scored 31 points, it wasn't enough. The Pistons won it, 93–74, as the rest of the Bulls went south again.

While Pippen said that "Michael knows he didn't carry us," the final game had to be a letdown. Horace Grant made just 3 of 17 shots, Pippen 1 of 10, Craig Hodges 3 of 13, B. J. Armstrong 1 of 8, and Bill Cartwright 3 of 9. No team can win with shooting like that. Not even a team with Michael Jordan.

Many Bulls' fans were still thinking about that final game when the 1990–91 season began. Why should this year be any different, they reasoned, the team hadn't really changed much. That was true. The Bulls picked up veterans Dennis Hopson and Cliff Levingston to help the bench. Otherwise, they had basically the same cast of characters as in the year before. But despite that awful seventh game with Detroit, the team had been very successful. Now, with the young players a year older, maybe this would be the year.

It would if Michael Jordan had anything to say about it. Michael was playing the same brilliant brand of basketball he had always played. If anything, he was going out of his way to get his teammates more involved in the offense. His scoring average was down slightly, though he still led the league. At the same time, Pippen was becoming a real all-star in his own right, Grant was improved, Cartwright was still steady and getting more help from Will Perdue. Paxson and B. J. Armstrong were doing a job at point guard.

There was little doubt as the season wore on that the Bulls had become one of the NBA's elite teams. In fact, they were close to having the best record in the league. And while Michael failed to reach the 50-point mark once during the year, his all-around game was so good, so controlled, that many felt it was his best season ever. In fact, he seemed to be truly enjoying himself on the court. His junior high coach, Fred Lynch, couldn't help noticing that very thing while watching Michael during a late-season game.

"The Bulls were playing Charlotte," Lynch said, "and my feeling was that Michael was just having fun playing the game. He was smiling a lot, just enjoying himself. Of course, it helps when you're up 15 or 20 as the Bulls were. But it still amazes me that night after night he's able to go out there and play at the same level. I think he'd play all 48 minutes every night if they'd let him."

The fun continued right until the end of the regular season. The Bulls won the Central Division title with a 61-21 mark, best record in franchise history. They also topped the defending-champion Pistons by 11 games and came within just two games of tying Portland for the best record in the league.

Michael again played all 82 games while averaging

31.5 points to take his fifth consecutive scoring title. He had help from Pippen, who averaged 17.8, and Grant, who was at 12.8. The two young forwards also played outstanding defense along with Michael. Then, as an added incentive during the playoffs, Michael was named the NBA's Most Valuable Player for the second time in his career. And there was absolutely no one who disputed the choice. That's how good he had been during the year. In fact, the vote was a landslide.

"He's the only player in the game who has no weaknesses," said Portland's veteran guard Danny Ainge, in a statement that seemed to perfectly sum up the essence of Michael Jordan. Michael himself was grateful for the award and obviously pleased to be chosen.

"This is well received by myself, my family, and my teammates," he said. "Most of the credit, though, should go to my teammates, who have stepped up and put us in this position. When a team wins, all the individual accolades follow."

When Michael received the award at halftime during one of the early playoff games, he asked his teammates to come out on the court with him. They were actually the ones who gave him the prize.

"It was a very touching moment for me," he said. "I've always wanted to simply be part of a team, and that's why I wanted them out there with me when I got the award. They have been part of it for the way they have played and it gave me the feel of a real family situation."

Michael also knew both he and the team had some unfinished business. They wanted a championship.

"But while I am very happy about receiving this award," he continued, "I want a championship more, and I feel our chances are greater than they've ever been."

It was as if this time he knew he would have help. The young players had matured and were finally in complete sync with their superstar leader. Despite some tendinitis in his knees (an occupational hazard), Michael was well rested. Coach Jackson had intentionally cut his minutes during the year, trying to keep him fresh for those times when extra effort was needed.

In the opening round the Bulls went up against the New York Knickerbockers and their superstar center, Patrick Ewing. But Bill Cartwright always played his former teammate tough, and the rest of the Knicks were no match for Michael and his improving teammates. The Bulls swept the Knicks three straight and hardly broke a sweat in the process. They looked strong and confident. Next they would have to meet a good Philadelphia 76ers team that had finished 44-38 in the regular season.

The Sixers were led by a great all-purpose player of their own, Charles Barkley, and had always had good success against the Bulls. In seven years the Sixers were 23-12 over the Bulls in the regular season, including a 3-1 edge in 1990–91. Many felt that this was the series in which Michael would have to assert himself, and his teammates would have to take a backseat. There was still little confidence in the other Bulls. Indiana's Reggie Miller had said earlier in the season, "Trade Michael Jordan and what do they have? Nothing."

That was a pretty rough assessment. But perhaps it was the Bulls' John Paxson who best described the nature of the team's problem.

"You have a player who can take over a game like nobody ever," Paxson said, "yet you have one who can get everyone involved. It's great to have a teammate like that. But try living up to it."

In other words, the pressure was on the other Bulls. Michael had always been willing to lessen his role. In effect, he would step aside for a few minutes and say, "Here, you guys do it." And if they didn't, he would race to the rescue, stronger than ever. In the eyes of most, that was the situation that had to change if the Bulls wanted to go all the way. But maybe it *was* changing. In one game against the Knicks, Michael left with the Bulls winning by 13. When he returned, his teammates had upped the lead to 21.

That's how things continued against the Sixers. With everyone contributing, the Bulls won the first two games handily, 105–92 and 112–100. Even when the Sixers returned home to win the third game 99–97, it was becoming increasingly obvious to everyone that this Chicago team was different. The entire club was playing with confidence. Michael was still the leader, still the man who would have the ball at crunch time. He had scored 46 in the third-game defeat. But if he was covered, Scottie Pippen was a solid second choice, and maybe in some circumstances, an equal choice.

It all came to the fore in the crucial fourth game. The Bulls took charge early, and if the Sixers were laying for Jordan, the strategy didn't work. When it ended, Chicago had a 101–85 victory and one of their best team efforts of the season. Horace Grant had 22 points and 11 rebounds, while Pippen hit for 20 points to go with 9 rebounds and 5 assists. Michael scored 25 and played outstanding defense on Sixer guard Hersey Hawkins. The Bulls resembled anything but a one-man team.

"It's hard when the media talks about us letting Michael down," Horace Grant said after the game. "I used to sit there reading that stuff and thinking, 'Jeez, it's not like we're not trying.' But it has gotten easier, and this year has been the best of all."

After that, the Bulls wasted no time dispensing with the Sixers. They won the next game, 100–95, to close out the series. In this one Michael was absolutely brilliant. He scored the Bulls' last 12 points, with 8 of them coming after the Sixers had rallied to erase a 13-point Bulls' lead to tie the score. Michael finished with 38 points (which was expected) and 19 big rebounds (which was not).

Now, for the third straight season, the Bulls were in the Eastern Conference finals. And sure enough, for a third straight time they would be facing the Detroit Pistons, who were trying to become the first team since the Celtics in the mid-1960s to win three straight NBA titles. This was also essentially the same club that had eliminated the Bulls the two previous seasons. Though the Pistons had been riddled by injuries during a good part of the regular season, they were still a dangerous ballclub. Unless the Bulls had really made that big step from being a good team to becoming a great team, they once again would have trouble winning.

While many predicted the Bulls would win the series, no one could have expected what took place. Chicago completely dominated the so-called Bad Boys from Detroit, doing the job at both ends of the court and doing it as a team. The Pistons might have been an aging ballclub, and their backcourt star, Isiah

Thomas, was banged up. But they were still an experienced, deep team and the two-time defending champions. That had to account for something.

"They're beatable," Michael had said before the series started. "We just have to find a way to beat them."

The opener had to be a tremendous shot in the arm for the Bulls. Like the Pistons, they were playing tremendous defense, but took just a scant lead, 68–65, into the final quarter. This time it wasn't Michael, but a pair of reserves, Craig Hodges and Cliff Levingston, who keyed a 13–7 run that brought the lead to 81–72. From there the Bulls coasted home to a 94–83 victory. Michael had just 22 points, but Pippen had 18 and Cartwright 16. Team effort? Most decidedly.

Game 2 was more of the same. The Bulls got continued help from reserves B. J. Armstrong, Hodges, Levingston, and Will Perdue to help key a second team effort, resulting in a 105–97 victory and a 2-0 lead. Now the clubs traveled to Detroit for the third game. If the Pistons were going to turn it around, it would have to be there.

Not this time. These were not the same Chicago Bulls who went south when the going got tough. Michael did have 33 points, 7 rebounds, and 7 assists in Game 3, but he had plenty of help. The Pistons made several runs at Chicago but could never overtake the Bulls' lead or get the team to crumble. A 113–107 victory gave Chicago a commanding 3-0 lead in the series.

Surprisingly, it was the Bulls' trapping defense that was doing much of the job. The *D* was taking the Pistons out of their set-up offense, and the starters were having trouble putting points on the board.

"It takes some believing for players to step up and realize they can make this thing happen," Michael said.

But the Bulls were believing. Even Coach Jackson was feeling it. "We took their best shot today," he said. And he was right. The fourth game wasn't even close. Chicago won it going away, 115–94, completing an improbable sweep and propelling themselves into the NBA's championship round for the first time ever. Once again it was a team effort. Michael had 29 points, Pippen 23, Grant 16, Paxson 12, and Levingston 10. It was the kind of balanced attack the team—and Michael—had always wanted. The Bulls were jubilant.

"I've got to give so much credit to Scottie Pippen, Horace Grant, and the rest of the supporting cast," Michael said, afterward. "This is a big step for the city and the fans. Now we go to the finals, and we'll do our best to win it."

Maybe it was Horace Grant, however, who expressed the prevailing feeling about the victory. "We wanted to beat Detroit so we could get the monkey off our back," he said.

That they did. While the Bulls awaited the winner of the Portland Trail Blazers–Los Angeles Lakers series, people already were asking Michael about playing against Laker star Magic Johnson.

"I guess everyone wants to see me play against Magic," Michael said. "What bothers me is that the matchup would take the spotlight off the team, and I don't want that to happen. If we play Portland, the emphasis will be on the team."

Michael obviously didn't want to lose what everyone had worked so hard to build. While it was

The final round of the 1990–91 playoffs produced the so-called dream matchup between Michael and the Lakers' Magic Johnson. But basketball is a team game and it was the team effort that carried the Bulls to victory. Here Michael has help from forward Horace Grant in stopping the Magic Man from penetrating to the hoop. *(AP/Wide World Photo)*

doubtful Michael or his teammates would allow that to happen, it was still a concern to him. That's how team-oriented Air Jordan had become. He didn't want anything to offset the delicate balance the team had finally achieved.

As it turned out, the Bulls went up against Magic and the Lakers after all. L.A. had used every bit of experience and guile to upset the favored Trail Blazers in six games. Many so-called experts also picked Magic and his mates to beat the Bulls. The reason was that many teams reaching the NBA finals for the first time just don't cut it in the championship round. The combination of inexperience and nerves often sabotages first-timers.

So when the series opened at a packed Chicago Stadium, opinions were still divided. Would the young Bulls prevail? Or would the older, slower Lakers find a way to play to their strengths and win?

There was an interesting connection between the two teams. Laker forwards James Worthy and Sam Perkins had been Michael's teammates at North Carolina, all three members of the national championship team of 1982. Now they were playing for the NBA title.

The first game was painfully close all the way. Though both teams scored liberally in the first quarter, the Bulls just couldn't get their running game in gear and seemed to play into the hands of the Lakers, who utilized a half-court game, preferring to post-up. Magic, Worthy, Perkins, and center Vlade Divac were all proficient at operating with their backs to the basket, taking the ball close in to the hoop, and getting good shots or drawing a foul.

Michael played well, hitting on a number of dunks and jump shots early on. He was also guarding Magic on defense and some felt the pressure at both ends of the court might tire him. It was a 30–29 game after one quarter, the Bulls on top, and 53–51 at the half, Chicago still up, by two. With their younger legs, the third period should have been the one in which the Bulls asserted themselves.

However, just the opposite happened—the Lakers continued to slow the pace. Suddenly the Bulls were rattled. Except for Michael, Chicago appeared tentative and unsure. The Lakers moved out to a 75–68 lead after three. Now the two teams got ready for the final 12 minutes of action. It was crunch time, the time when Michael normally took over.

The script came close to a storybook ending for the Bulls—but not quite. With their superstar leading the charge, the Bulls clawed their way back into the game. Even after he picked up his fifth foul with 5:31 left, Michael continued to play hard. Finally the Bulls edged ahead, 91–89. Now they had possession again with less than 30 seconds left. It was their chance to put the game away.

As expected, Michael got the ball. With the clock moving down past the 25-second mark, he tried a short jumper from the right side. It banked off the glass, but missed. The Lakers rebounded and moved downcourt. Magic spotted Sam Perkins open on the right side behind the three-point line and whipped the ball to him. Perkins unloaded his lefty jumper and it went in! The Lakers suddenly had a 92–91 lead with just 14 seconds left.

All 18,676 fans at Chicago Stadium knew just who would take the final Chicago shot. Michael surprised everyone by trying to pass inside, but the ball was swatted away. The Bulls had still another chance with nine seconds left. This time Michael dribbled to the left side of the foul circle and let go with about a 17-foot jumper. For a split second it seemed to be headed through the iron. Then it kicked out! The Bulls fouled L.A.'s Byron Scott in the scramble for the rebound, and Scott hit one of two free throws with just over two seconds left. The Bulls couldn't get another shot off. It was over. The Lakers won it, 93–91, taking a 1-0 lead in the series and also grabbing the home-court advantage from the Bulls. The loss shocked everyone.

Although he had scored 36 points, Michael had missed two shots at the end that enabled the Lakers to win.

"My last two shots, that was the game all the way around," said Michael afterward. "I was wide open on that last one, and it felt good when I let it go. But that's the nature of the game. There's no reason to panic."

Aside from Michael, however, Scottie Pippen with 19 points was the only other Bull in double figures. Michael said what everyone else was thinking.

"I hope in the next game my supporting cast can hit some shots."

It wasn't meant as a dig, but rather as a wake-up call. He didn't want his teammates falling into old habits, standing around and watching Air Jordan do it. Like everyone else, Michael also knew that the second game was crucial. If the Bulls lost again, they would have to travel to Los Angeles for the next three games, down 2-0.

"The season is right now," said Michael. "We know

we've got to win. Everything has been leading up to Game 2. We've had important games, like last year in Detroit, but nothing compares to this."

Coach Jackson made one big change for the second contest—he decided to let Pippen guard Magic. The Chicago forward was a little bigger and heavier than Michael, and almost as quick. He could be more physical and maybe free Michael up for a little more late-game offense.

But the Lakers knew Michael would get his points. L.A. coach Mike Dunleavy acknowledged that the Lakers "weren't trying to give him 36 [points]. He's just so good, he gets them."

But if his teammates continued to falter, Michael couldn't do it alone. As Laker guard Byron Scott said, "If he can go for 40, 45, and Pippen gets 17, that's OK. If [Jordan] scores that many points, it means the other guys aren't doing it."

In the opening minutes of Game 2, Michael was creating a different mood for his team. Instead of shooting, he dished the ball off every chance he had. In fact, it took him a full 18 minutes, just six minutes short of halftime, to put up his third shot from the floor. He wanted his teammates to know he still felt they could do the job. It might have been a bit of a gamble, but it was something Michael felt he had to do. And it worked!

The game was close for the first half, but all the Bulls were responding. Horace Grant had 14 points by intermission. John Paxson was hitting his jumper from both sides. Pippen was not only doing a fine job on Magic, but was also scoring off the break. The Bulls moved out to a 48–43 lead at the half, and they were just getting started. By the end of the third quarter it was a rout.

Convinced that his teammates were now relaxed and fully involved in the game, Michael shot more. Within minutes it was the Air Jordan show again. Everything he was throwing up was going in—drives, jumpers, and his patented electrifying slam-dunks. Led by Michael, the Bulls scored 38 points in the third period, opening up their lead to a comfortable 86–69.

Michael was on an incredible run. He would hit 13 straight shots during his third- and fourth-period rampage. Then, early in the final session, he produced one of his unique moments. He drove down the lane, extending the ball straight out in his right hand as if he were going in for another dunk. As he flew through the air, he saw Sam Perkins sliding over to stop the shot.

Just as he began falling forward, Michael suddenly flipped the ball from his right hand to his left and on his downward flight flipped up an underhand scoop shot. The spin on the ball was perfect. It kissed off the glass and went in. The capacity crowd erupted and so did Michael, pumping his fist through the air several times, then high-fiving a couple of teammates as he went back down the court.

"When Michael has it going like that, that's when all of his creativity is going too," said Magic Johnson afterward. "He gets the feeling of [being] unstoppable, invincible, that whole thing."

Both Michael and the Bulls were indeed unstoppable. They ran out a 107–86 victory to even the series at a game apiece. In the process the Bulls shot a record 61.7 percent from the floor. Michael was an incredible 15 for 18, scoring 33 points. This time, however, he had help. Grant and Pippen had 20 each, while Paxson hit on all eight of his shots, for 16 points. In addition to his scoring, Michael added 13 assists and 7 rebounds for an all-around brilliant game.

Even the defensive change had worked. Scottie Pippen had done a fine job on Magic, holding the Laker star to just 4-for-13 shooting from the floor and 14 points. The only hint of controversy was an accusation by some of the Lakers that Michael was taunting them, rubbing it in when the Bulls began to roll. They were apparently annoyed by a palms-up gesture Michael made after hitting a jumper during his incredible run of 13 straight shots.

"I wasn't saying anything to any of their players," Michael said. "It was more or less my self-motivation and excitement at what I did."

As the teams headed for the Great Western Forum in Los Angeles for the next three games, it was the Lakers who had to regroup. The tone of the series seemed to turn, along with the momentum. The Bulls began to get the feeling they had in the Eastern Conference finals against Detroit. It was a feeling that they couldn't be stopped.

But there was one more test the Bulls had to pass. Game 3 in Los Angeles was a battle and a test of character at the same time. It was tied at 25 after one quarter. By halftime, just a point separated the two teams, the Bulls leaving the floor with a 48–47 lead. Then came the crucial third quarter. Early in the period the Bulls had moved to a 52–49 advantage. That was when the Lakers caught fire.

Led by Magic and center Divac, Los Angeles ran off 12 straight points in the midst of an 18–2 explosion that had their fans in an uproar. Not even Michael could buy a basket during the L.A. surge, which brought the score up to 67–54. But just when it looked like Chicago would collapse, the Bulls fought back, narrowing the margin to 72–66 by the end of the period. Michael had hit just one of six shots in the session, so the Chicago comeback was even more significant. They had done it almost without their superstar.

Midway through the final quarter the Bulls pulled even at 74. It was pointed out that during the last eight minutes, eight different players had scored for the Bulls, and Michael contributed just a pair of free throws, more evidence that they were doing it as a team.

From there it was nip and tuck. With just 11 seconds left, the Bulls were up by a single point at 90–89. But Laker center Vlade Divac then made an awkward bank shot from in close and was fouled. The three-point play gave the Lakers a 92–90 lead with 10.9 seconds remaining.

Though Michael had hit just 2 of 10 shots in the second half, he still got the ball with the game on the line. He waited until the clock was down to five seconds, then made his move. It was a 14-foot jumper over the outstretched hand of Divac, and it tied the game with 3.4 seconds left. The Lakers couldn't score in the remaining time, and the game went into over-time.

In the OT, Michael forgot about his poor shooting. It was still a close game, tied at 96–96, when he canned a nifty reverse layup with 1:45 left. From there, the Bulls rolled. Michael hit another layup and a pair of free throws as Chicago took the game, 104–96, giving the Bulls a 2-1 lead in the series.

Though Michael wound up with 29 points, he was just 11 for 28 from the floor, poor shooting for him. But Grant had 22, Pippen 19, and reserve Cliff Levingston chipped in with 10. The Bulls were doing it as a team.

Game 4 wasn't even close. The Bulls were down by a point after one period, but then ran to a 52–44 halftime lead. By the end of three it was 74–58, as the Chicago defense held the Lakers to just 14 third-quarter points. From there, the Bulls cruised to a 97–82 victory and a 3-1 lead in the series. Michael had 28 in that one, with balanced support from his mates. The Lakers knew they were in big trouble.

"I never dreamed this would happen," said Magic Johnson. "You anticipate a great series. You didn't anticipate anything like this. I can't feel bad because they're just giving us a nice butt-kicking."

There were more problems for the Lakers. Worthy had left Game 4 with a sprained ankle, while guard Byron Scott, already mired in a terrible shooting slump, suffered a badly bruised shoulder late in the contest. Sam Perkins, who had been the hero in Game 1, hit just one of 15 shots in Game 4. It was obvious to nearly everyone that the Bulls and Michael Jordan were on the brink of their first-ever championship.

Michael couldn't have been happier that his teammates were playing so well. He felt that people would stop looking at the Bulls as a one-man team and that they would also see him as more than a one-dimensional player. Despite being named Defensive Player of the Year several years earlier and making the all-defensive team a number of times, many still viewed him as primarily an explosive scorer.

"What people are seeing in this series," he said, "is

that I do play an all-around game. Maybe this will open some people's eyes that I'll do whatever is needed, whether it's shooting, rebounding. Whatever."

And when someone mentioned championship, Michael said simply, "What we're about to accomplish is something very few people get the opportunity to do and that a lot of people said I wouldn't get the chance to do. I want it. I can smell it. And I can taste it."

With Worthy and Scott out of the lineup, the Lakers started two youngsters, forward Elden Campbell and guard Tony Smith. Though little used before Game 5, both played extremely well, responding to the urgings and pinpoint passing of Magic, who began rolling up the assists from the outset. In fact, if it hadn't been for the newfound balance and tenacity of the Bulls, the Lakers might very well have taken control of the ballgame.

With both Campbell and Smith contributing to the scoring, L.A. trailed by just two, 27–25, after the first quarter, then played the Bulls better than ever in the second, taking a 49–48 lead into the locker room. It was more of the same in the third, the two teams playing to a standoff. In fact, when the horn sounded to end the third session, the game was dead even at 80. The final 12 minutes would decide if the Bulls were to emerge as champions or whether the series would have to return to Chicago for a sixth tilt.

Once again the two teams battled it out. The Bulls were getting big games from Jordan and Pippen, while Magic, Perkins, and the youngster Campbell led L.A. With just 3:54 left, the game was deadlocked again, this time at 93. That's when the Bulls suddenly got a lift from an unlikely source. With the Laker defense sagging toward the middle to stop Jordan and Pippen, guard John Paxson was repeatedly left open on the wings. Seeing the open man, the other Bulls delivered the ball and Paxson began connecting on long jumpers.

At one point he hit three straight to just about break it open. In the final 3:54, Paxson scored 10 points to help put the icing on the cake. The surging Bulls had come through once again. Only, this time it was for all the marbles. They won the game, 108–101, and were champions of the basketball world—at last!

In the final game Michael had scored 30 points, second to Pippen's 32. Paxson wound up with 20 and had hit a torrid 9 of 12 shots from the field. It was another super team effort, negating Magic's 20 assists, 22 points from Perkins, and 21 from Campbell. The Bulls had shown everyone they were true champions, and no one was happier than Michael Jordan.

For openers, Michael was named the Most Valuable Player of the finals. He had averaged 31.2 points, 6.4 rebounds, and a surprising 10.4 assists. In the locker room he fell to his knees, clutching the championship trophy. Even his arch rival, Magic Johnson, couldn't help being moved by the emotional scene he witnessed when he went in to congratulate the winners.

"When I saw Michael after the game, there were tears in his eyes," Magic said. "You hear so much talk about him as an individual player, but he's proved everyone wrong with this championship."

Michael himself was so full of emotion that it was sometimes difficult for him to speak. There were so many things to say, because he had waited so long.

The moment of triumph! Michael raises his arms in victory as the Bulls close out the Lakers, 108–101, to win their first-ever NBA Championship in five games. *(AP/Wide World Photo)*

"This means so much to the team and the city of Chicago," he said, as he hugged his parents and his wife. "It was a seven-year struggle. We started from scratch, at the bottom. But every year we worked harder and harder, until we got it. Now we can get rid of the stigma of a one-man team. We did it as a team all season long. I played my game, but with their efforts, we were a better team. We knew Magic wouldn't go down without a fight. We had to take it from him.

"I don't know if I'll ever have this same feeling again. What you see is the emotion of hard work. I never thought I'd be this emotional or show this emotion publicly. But right now I just don't mind."

He had tears in his eyes as he spoke. And while Michael continued to emphasize the title as a team victory, others marveled at the talent and character of Michael Jordan.

"He's the finest athlete I've ever seen in the NBA," said Jack Ramsay, a former NBA coach and longtime observer of the basketball scene. "He's not only a great player, but a class individual as well."

Play-by-play announcer Marv Albert said the victory would silence doubters who had wondered over the years whether a team dominated by Michael Jordan could win. Albert's color commentator, former NBA coach Mike Fratello, said that Michael "sacrificed as soon as his supporting cast blossomed. He's always been willing to spread the wealth around."

That was true in more ways than one. There's a commercial involving a trip to a famous amusement park that is traditionally filmed immediately after a professional team wins the championship. It usually involves the star player, asking him what he plans to do now that he's a champion. The answer, of course, is that he is going to the amusement park. Michael refused to do the commercial unless the rest of the Bulls were included as well. That's how it was done, as "we" rather than "I."

John Paxson, who played such an instrumental role in the Bulls' victory, related his feelings about Michael and might well have been expressing the feelings of the entire team.

"I accepted a long time ago that Michael is the greatest athlete in the sport, maybe in the world," said Paxson. "And you've got to accept your role. Michael's challenged me at times. The great ones do that."

Now the great one was also a champion. Asked what he wanted next, Michael mentioned two things—the first will be difficult to come by, the second a little easier, perhaps.

"I'd like some privacy," Michael Jordan said, "and then another championship."

Michael Jordan is a man with his life in perspective. He has learned to accept the fact that he is a celebrity and role model, something he admits isn't always easy.

"I do it because people expect it," he said. "But it's tough to be in a situation where every mistake you make will be magnified 10 times. People tend to put you on a pedestal, and that isn't easy. Yes, I resent it some of the time."

But Michael has played the role well—as well as

any athlete could under the circumstances. There's also little doubt about Michael's place in the history of his sport. His achievements so far have assured him of that.

Yet even before the Bulls went on to win the championship, Michael was philosophical. He knew nothing was certain, that the Bulls could lose as well as win. He said then he would be able to accept it either way.

"To lose would be disappointing," he said. "But my career will never be a disappointment. The things I've gone through, the people I've met, and the things we've done as a team will always stay with me. No matter what happens this year or in the future, I won't look back, and I'll never say my career was tarnished."

Michael's philosophy reflects the maturing attitude of a very successful man. He once called basketball the "best job in the world." But even as far back as 1989, he knew that an injury or illness could suddenly take his skills from him. If that happened, he would be ready to deal with it.

"If I lost my talent tomorrow," he said, "I'd say I had a great time and move on. I live for today but plan for the future."

Basketball fans the world over can only hope that doesn't happen soon. They never seem to get enough of the player with the flopping tongue, flying feet, and moves too numerous to count. The words spoken several years ago by Magic Johnson may be the most appropriate of all, for they seem to ring even more true with each passing year. Said Magic, even before the Bulls whipped the Lakers for the championship:

"There's Michael, and then there's everybody else."

An emotional Michael Jordan meets the press in the Chicago locker room following the Bulls' fifth-game triumph over the Lakers to take the NBA crown. Winning the championship had been Michael's goal for himself and his teammates from the day he entered the NBA. *(AP/Wide World Photo)*

MICHAEL JORDAN'S COLLEGE
AND PROFESSIONAL STATS

COLLEGE—NORTH CAROLINA

Season	G	FGs	Pct.	FTs	Pct.	Reb.	Asst.	Pts.	Avg.
1981–82	34	191	53.4	78	72.2	149	61	460	13.5
1982–83	36	282	53.5	123	73.6	197	56	721	20.0
1983–84	31	247	55.1	113	77.9	163	64	607	19.6
Totals	101	720	54.0	314	74.8	509	181	1,788	17.7

NBA REGULAR SEASON

Season	G	FGs	Pct.	FTs	Pct.	Reb.	Asst.	Pts.	Avg.
1984–85	82	837	51.5	630	84.5	534	481	2,313	28.2
1985–86	18	150	45.7	105	84.0	64	53	408	22.7
1986–87	82	1,098	48.2	833	85.7	430	377	3,041	37.1
1987–88	82	1,069	53.5	723	84.1	449	485	2,868	35.0
1988–89	81	966	53.8	674	85.0	652	650	2,633	32.5
1989–90	82	1,034	52.6	593	84.8	565	519	2,753	33.6
1990–91	82	990	53.9	571	85.1	492	453	2,580	31.5
Totals	509	6,144	51.3	4,129	84.7	3,186	3,018	16,596	32.6

NBA PLAYOFFS

Season	G	FGs	Pct.	FTs	Pct.	Reb.	Asst.	Pts.	Avg.
1984–85	4	34	43.6	48	82.8	23	34	117	29.3
1985–86	3	48	50.5	34	87.2	19	17	131	43.7
1986–87	3	35	41.7	35	89.7	21	18	107	35.7
1987–88	10	138	53.0	86	86.8	71	47	363	36.3
1988–89	17	199	51.0	183	79.9	119	130	591	34.8
1989–90	16	219	51.4	133	83.6	115	109	587	36.7
1990–91	17	197	52.4	125	84.5	108	142	529	31.1
Totals	70	870	49.1	644	84.9	476	497	2,425	34.6